My Wolf and Me

A NOVEL

By India R Adams

Dedicated to Kirsten 1936-2015
This book was her favorite
I love you, mama

PREFACE

T HE FLAME'S SHADOWS DANCE ACROSS my face as I watch our
fallen burn in the fire we lit. Ashes of their remains float up into
the cold winter wind, never to be seen again. My feet in the snow
no longer feel cold, nor does the evening air.

Memories of the love that withstood the test of time and that brought
me here grace me as the flame's shadows dance across my face.

Chapter One

Imaginations and Reality

My mother—happily cooking in her humble kitchen—was unaware of how far her young, adventurous child would wander off, playing outside, daring the world to shock her. I didn't realize it then, but that was exactly what the world would do: show me a reality that shouldn't exist but does, and did for a while in the woods behind my childhood home.

The warm sun shone down on me as I, once again, triumphantly journeyed through the forest. My worn trail to my make-believe castle was where I first met the two magnificent wolves who would soon deliver my destiny. Even though I was only six, their beauty awed me. Instead of being afraid, I believed my imagination had given me another gift.

Woods were not frightening for me. In the daylight, they were a magical place for me to investigate, experiment, be daring, and make believe. Of course, nighttime was a whole different period of mystery, which I willingly left to the adults. My imagination was so profound, reality often didn't exist for me. I invented a world to live out the boundless possibilities my overactive mind developed.

To my younger self, the smaller wolf seemed gentle, motherly, with her golden-brown fur and her kind brown eyes. The massive wolf beside her appeared stern and far too serious with his jet-black fur and haunting gray eyes.

"Hi," I excitedly greeted them. "My name is Marlena."

The black wolf did not seem to share my excitement. His body lowered as if ready to pounce. The brown wolf ignored him and gaped at me, as if surprised to see me wandering the expansive forest by myself.

"Would you like to see my castle?" I innocently asked.

The black wolf took two steps away from my path. The gentle wolf whimpered, not following. He turned his large snout back to her and blew air out before coming back to her side.

I observed his aggravated nose puff. "Do you need a tissue? I don't have any, but you could use my sleeve if you want to. I won't tell my mommy."

Dark-gray eyes regarded me, possibly in disbelief.

I shrugged at his loss. "Then let's go see my castle."

I was tickled pink to look back and see the two weary wolves following me, one more enthusiastically than the other. As we traveled, I informed them of crucial details. "It's no ordinary castle made of chocolate. No, those melt in the sun. Mine is special because it is under the protective spell of the witch, Coco-Matilda." I looked back at them and grinned. "Coco-Matilda loves chocolate, too."

At the end of the trail was my kingdom. "We're here!"

Two majestic wolves stood and stared at the unadorned boulders and tree limbs I considered the best playground ever.

"I know! Pretty amazing, right?" I hopped onto my castle and immediately pointed out all the rooms. "This is the kitchen where food almost as good as my mommy's and is made by elves. Here is my bedroom. It's the best because I'm queen." I froze as I had an epiphany. I pointed to my new friends. "I know who you are. My new guards! Castle guards!"

After another blow out the snout, I advised the male wolf, "You should see a doctor."

I was blissfully unaware that perhaps I should be playing with other boys and girls, but we didn't live in town, so we had no close neighbors. And stay-at-home parents were too busy minding their land and belongings to set up play dates. In this rural area, children without siblings or family nearby learned to entertain themselves.

I didn't mind being on my own, and my new companions didn't seem to like company anyway. They were excellent at their job. The Chocolate Castle Guards always looked around, suspicious of any movement or sounds. I fed my guards wonderful food—sticks, leaves, and pebbles—cooked by the elves as reward for their work well done. I received a snout blow from one wolf and a gentle lick from the other.

After hours of playing, the black wolf took single guard duty as the brown wolf rested in the sun. Becoming a little sleepy myself, I sat down and decided the kind wolf would make a great pillow. Laying my head on her belly, I said, "Wow, you ate too much breakfast. Your tummy is huge!" Another blow exited the black wolf's nose.

And so time went by. Every day, I met with my wolves, who waited patiently—well, one waited patiently as the other paced—for me on the path to my castle. Then one day, they weren't there. As queen, I had many duties, such as firing the Chocolate Castle Guards for missing work. A few weeks later, they finally returned with a precious little gray wolf tagging along. All was forgiven, and I rejoiced in my imagination's new addition. "You had a baby!"

I ran toward them but stopped when I saw the puppy hide behind his mother's hind legs. I knelt down and sat on my feet. "Aw, did I scare you? I'm sorry, little fella. I promise I won't hurt you."

The black wolf seemed extra alert, circling with his snout sniffing the air and his ears perked high. The mother wolf stepped behind her pup and nudged him toward me. I waited patiently for the proper introduction. Her tongue swiping my cheek seemed to be what the puppy needed to witness.

The puppy sniffed my knees as I held still for him.

"May I pet you, little fella?" My hand slowly reached and paused for more sniffing inspections. When he began sniffing the other hand resting on my knee, I slowly touched the top of his head. He froze… then pushed his head into my palm, seeming to enjoy the sensation. "Oh, that feels good, huh?"

My resting hand joined and scruffed under his chin. A tail wagged rapidly, and he practically crawled up my body to lick my cheeks as I petted him freely with praise. "What a good boy! I think you like some lovin'. Dontcha, little fella?"

When I had the chance to study his adorable face, I saw the most unique gray eyes in the whole world. They were much lighter than his father's, and they had rather creative white speckles through them, resembling clouds in the sky. Those eyes became a part of my soul that day.

The little wolf with wonderful eyes became my best friend within minutes. We skipped—well, *I* skipped as he chased. We played tag and fetch for hours. His parents, who were now affectionately and appropriately named Mother Wolf and Father Wolf, followed us closely. As always, one seemed at ease, the other far too tense.

When their baby wolf became tired, we were both nudged. "Where are we going?" I asked, until we ended up in an open cave. "Ohhhhh, wow!" There were leaves and debris on the stone ground that I imagined to be the underground world that singing snakes called home. Moss growing up the walls was the rope I needed to escape the musical snakes when they were hungry.

I adored the puppy breath blowing across my face as we lay together on the dirty cave floor. Once still, the puppy fell asleep, and his heavy breathing lulled me to the point where I drifted off myself. Mother and Father Wolf sat at the opening of the cave, studying the surroundings.

Since Mother and Father Wolf could not speak, I understood when they could not tell me their new baby's name. Since there was no obstacle I could not overcome, I gave him a name instead of pouting over the language barrier. And because my furry friend roamed with me every day, all through the forest...

"I know what I'll name you," I said with much enthusiasm. "Romy."

It was a proud day.

Father Wolf, who on all fours, stood as tall as I was, snorted with his never-ending cold. Mother Wolf proudly licked me; I knew she was pleased.

Romy grew at a drastic rate and, on all fours, was as tall as my hip in what felt like a few weeks. At the end of every play day, I dreaded leaving my best friend to go home and be forced into a tub to wash off the "grime," as my mother so delicately put it.

Mother and Father Wolf watched over Romy and me as we both handled the extremely serious Chocolate Castle business that needed attention, such as floods in the castle kitchen and fairies needing guidance to resolve arguments. Of course, I did all the talking, which bothered me not one bit, since talking was a favorite activity of mine. My *only* problem with my talking was how it would trigger Father Wolf's nose issues.

Romy never found the castle dilemmas boring or repetitive as we gloriously saved the day every day. No, he found castle business as urgent and important as I did. One day, when his father growled and took off deeper into the woods, leaving Mother Wolf behind, Romy and I were sure he also had to go and save the day.

Some days that need saving aren't supposed to be saved, no matter how desperately we want it.

When Father Wolf failed to return, Mother Wolf tucked Romy and me away in our napping cave. Normally, Romy and I pretended that the old cave was my castle's secret, underground tunnel that we needed once a day for nap time when Romy and I were invaded by Martians, who *unfortunately,* would catch up to us *every day* and force us to sleep with their green Martian potions. But on this day, Romy wasn't willing to play Martian takeover and was only paying attention to his mother. His alert gray eyes watched her pace the cave's entrance while we sat together.

My human intuition was the last to realize something was drastically wrong. I found myself turning to Romy for comfort. I looked up to the wolf that now sat taller than I did and clung to him as the veil of my imagination began to deteriorate. My magical, make-believe world dissipated in front of my eyes, and the underground tunnel—where I used to run to save our lives—was truly a cold cave. It was at that very moment, when reality showed itself, that Romy became the most important entity in my life. Something deep in my heart made me realize that he most likely would always be. And with that sense of change, Romy was no longer a part of my imagination. How *real* he truly was became evident, as did the seriousness of our situation.

Mother Wolf released a long exhale through her nose then came to stand in front of Romy and stared at him. They communicated as I had witnessed many times but had not really studied till now—now that my imagination could no longer fool me into thinking my wolf was pretend.

His head bobbed as his answer to his mother, and then he leaned toward me. Whatever he was telling his mother was what she must have wanted to hear because she nuzzled her face to his, licked me, and ran out of the cave. To where? I didn't know. Romy stayed by my side, not leaving me once, even when the sun began to set. I felt as if it was falling from the sky. Father and Mother Wolf had yet to return, and for the first time, Romy and I were left in the dark, alone.

Cozied up to his gray fur because the temperature was falling, I quietly said, "Romy? My mommy says I have to be home by dark."

Sad little clouded eyes looked at me. I was sure if Romy were human he would cry.

Leaving my best friend alone felt so wrong to my innocent, young mind. So I didn't.

I chose to stay and deal with the spanking that was surely to come for my disobedience. I put my arms around my wolf. "Okay, Romy. I'll stay with you."

We sat together, side by side, heart by heart, watching the sun... disappear.

I don't know if it took minutes or hours for Mother Wolf to return, but our thudding hearts didn't get the reprieve we hoped for, not when watching Mother Wolf half crawl and half drag her wounded body to the cave's entrance. Romy and I were both up to our feet and paws, running to the severely injured Mother Wolf.

I can still hear his whimpering to this day.

And I still feel the utter shock when I helplessly watched her collapse to the ground and turn into... a human.

Chapter Two

Howling in the Distance

BEING RIPPED FROM A FANTASY world and thrown into a true nightmare with mystical boundaries would have confused and possibly tormented any human above a certain age. Me? It just seemed to confirm that the world was *truly* the magical place I believed it to be.

Mother Wolf's brown eyes opened, and she weakly called, "Sebastian." Her voice was warm and tender, even in such a state.

I didn't know whose name that was, but Romy kept crying out, a little apprehensive with his mother's new form. Slowly, he approached and sniffed her. Then he tenderly nudged her with his snout, as if recognizing her scent. Mother Wolf's eyes closed, and she tried to smile as her son licked her cheek, but she stopped and curled into a fetal position, grunting in pain.

I knelt in front of her.

Shakily, Mother Wolf reached for her son again. "Sebastian... I'm so sorry... your father—"

I was desperate to know what had happened, but she stopped talking to cough up blood. Even as young as I was, I knew what that meant.

"Y-your father... has passed."

Romy might have been a wolf, but he became more frantic with every word she spoke.

"I too... must pass..."

Romy's heart-wrenching whimpers forced tears down my cheeks. I cried for my friend, who could not form such things as tears.

Mother Wolf's face paled rapidly. "B-be strong, my son. I'm so sorry to leave you... so soon. You have more to come... in your bright future." She looked at me for the very first time with her *human* eyes. "Dear Marlena, you are... so special. When my son was born, I knew you could... teach him... a language I had... to hide from. I know you can do what... I ask of you. Please—" Coughing up more blood interrupted her, and I was afraid she would not get the chance to finish. "Please look after my son—your Romy. Keep his secret close to your heart always. H-he has much to learn and needs you."

I nodded as I cried. "I will. I love him."

A gracious smile passed her lips, shining past the smears of dirt and blood. "I know you do. He can't tell you yet... but he loves you, too."

"Yet?" I sniffled while wiping my nose on the back of my hand because my mother wasn't there to give me a tissue.

"Yes, Sebastian will come to his change... and might be scared. You don't need to be scared though... and remember, he will never hurt you. Remind him of these simple words when... his time comes..." She proceeded to give me information that made no sense to my young mind, but I promised to remember every word. I tried so hard.

Times come in your life that you wish you could avoid, run from, but you can't. They come, and you have to bear and live through them.

As her breathing became more and more labored, Romy became more and more panicked, pacing, nudging, whimpering. When her hand reached for his paw, he froze and watched her. The blood pooling on the cave floor told us her last moment had come.

"There are ones who belong to you... but you are not of... age or size to enter the pack. Please don't search for them... Stay with your Marle—" She didn't have the strength to finish my name.

Romy stood by his mother's side as her eyes closed.

I numbly sat on the ground at the cave entrance and watched as the moon shone down on Romy, caressing his loneliness as if trying to blanket him from such devastating pain. Romy rolled his shoulders back as he faced the sky and then painfully howled into the night.

As young ones do, Romy and I soon gave in to our exhaustion and fell asleep, clutching each other the only way wolf and child can. His soft winter coat gave me all the heat I needed for my human body to survive the chill.

I didn't wake to the man rummaging around in the woods with a flashlight, not even as he approached the cave. I woke to a growl I'd never heard before that sad night.

My eyes opened to see Romy standing protectively over my body.

With a flashlight shining in my eyes, I could not see who was frozen in fear, but I soon knew who it was when I heard, "No! Don't hurt my daughter."

I tried to get to my feet but was challenged with a wolf over me. "Daddy?"

Instantly, Romy stopped growling and lowered his head, letting me up.

"Marlena, please don't move. The wolf will hurt you."

With my hand on my wolf, I said, "Romy? He would *never* hurt me."

My father's jaw dropped. "This *wolf* is your *imaginary* friend Romy, the Roamer?"

I nodded proudly, smiling. "Look! He's real!"

His hand shook as he gestured to me. "I see that. Come to Daddy, little girl."

I ran and jumped into my father's arms, noticing he was not as warm as Romy, but loving his embrace never the less. My father hugged me tightly as he sighed.

"Daddy, Romy's daddy is dead like his mommy. He needs to live with us now."

"Little girl, he's not a dog. H-he's a wolf—"

My father struggled to hold me, but I squirmed out of his arms and ran to Romy. I stood in front of my wolf with a scowl on my cold face. Pointing a tiny finger to my father, I scolded him. "Romy is my best friend, and that was his mother." When I looked at her, I was shocked to see Mother Wolf in wolf form again. But then I remembered she was probably trying to protect Romy's secret, as she had asked me to do. "A-and he is now all alone. He needs me!"

I suppose my father would have agreed to anything to have me back in his arms. "Okay, little girl. Just come back to me." His blue eyes watched me, anxiously waiting.

Back in his arms, I learned my father had no intention of taking a wild animal home with us, and there was nothing I could say to convince him otherwise.

Being forcefully carried away, I cried, screamed, and sobbed for my friend. Back at the cave, Romy howled. He had just lost everything, including me.

At home, my mother tried to soothe her hysterical child in the bathtub. Soon, she gave up and tried putting me to bed. It was so late, and I was so tired that my body surrendered. Only my pink lamp on my night stand was lit. My white floral quilt was tucked over my lightly trembling body. I continued to cry quietly as my mother caressed my head.

Romy still howled in the distance.

"Everett, is he getting closer?" my mother, lying in bed with me, whispered to my father.

He looked out my second-floor bedroom window to our backyard. "Yeah, sure sounds like it."

That was when I remembered his sense of smell. My Romy was going to find his way to me.

When my parents went to sleep in their bedroom because I'd smartened up and faked falling asleep, I grabbed my blanket and pillow and snuck down the stairs, headed for the back porch of our simple log cabin. I had the only bedroom upstairs. My parents slept downstairs in the front of the house.

At the bottom of the stairs, I checked for the scary creatures of the night, but all I saw was a dark living room to my left. Only a light glow remained in the fireplace. To my right was our small kitchen, where I could usually find my mother, and our cozy eating area. Ten feet in front of me was my destination—the back door.

It was a humble home, but enough for a hardworking man and a stay-at-home mom to live very happily. My father was proud and loved his little family with all his heart.

I adjusted my blanket and pillow to prepare for my sprint and took off running, my bare feet pitter-patting on the old wooden floors. At the back door, I hesitated. Well, it was dark and scary, but when I tippy-toed and looked through the door's window, I saw my furry friend sniffing the back porch steps. I hesitated no longer. I snuck outside quietly to a sad wolf that seemed to want to be by my side, but apparently wasn't trusting the unknown objects I called stairs. I had to coax him to me while he sniffed each step, the blue flowerpot, and the bristly mat as though everything was foreign to him.

I guessed it was.

Soon, he calmed, and we hunkered down for the night. With my back to the outer wall of my house, I lay down on my side. Romy curled in front of me with his head on the pillow we shared, and I snuggled to his furry back after covering us both with my blanket.

After finding Romy and me on the porch sleeping together three mornings in a row, my parents felt they had no choice. Romy was officially welcomed to the family and became our... dog—well, *wolf.*

My mother was as reluctant to allow an animal inside the home as the animal was to come *into* the home. He sniffed and kept his tail down, debating whether or not it was safe. I looked around and realized Romy had never seen a house before. He knew nothing that belonged to humans other than what he saw with me, which was, well, just *me.*

I knelt down in front of the stairs that led to my bedroom, being patient during Romy's examination of the open back doorway. Gray eyes stared at me as he stayed on the porch and sniffed and sniffed. I smiled and waited and waited.

Romy stopped sniffing, looked at me again, and paused. Time seemed to slow as we stared at each other. Something Romy saw made him cross the barrier and enter my home—now our home—and lick my face.

My mom protested that evening, but I won, and Romy got to sleep in bed with me. He hated the blanket, but I was stubborn, and he waited until I fell asleep to crawl out from underneath the heated cover.

People should follow children's examples and live without worry, love and appreciate everything around them, and most of all, accept what has transpired and move forward. Romy was the prime example of such courage.

The next morning, it was still dark when I woke with no Romy in my bed. Sitting up, I saw a sad wolf sitting by my window, staring into the woods. I wondered what he hoped to see. I thought of his mother and knew how sad I would be to not be able to see my mommy anymore. Remembering my Uncle Trey passing away a few months before, I knew what we had to do.

With a blanket and a shovel that was bigger than I was dragging behind us, my wolf and I went deep into the woods to bury his mother.

Romy ran to her and sniffed the wolf body that no longer carried a soul. I tried not to pay attention to the evidence of how nature works, the marks of smaller animals finding a meal. She was very heavy, but I managed to get the blanket under her. I grabbed one corner, Romy bit the other, and we both pulled as hard as we could, dragging his mother to where the earth was softer so we could lay her to rest.

While I used the monstrous shovel as best I could, Romy lay with Mother Wolf. I believe he wanted every last moment he could have with her, alive or dead. As the morning sun rose, the glow made Mother Wolf look as if she was peacefully sleeping, half covered in a blanket. It was a kind way for a son to see his mother for the last time.

Being so young and small, I could only dig a shallow grave. Once done, Romy and I pulled on the blanket and laid his mother to rest. The little mound of dirt covering her was all there was left to see—but not to feel. Romy sat next to the mound, not ready to leave her, so I sat next to my wolf and waited for him to find some peace. I don't know how long we sat side by side, leaning on each other, and it didn't matter. I would've stayed next to him forever.

CHAPTER THREE

LET A WOLF BE A WOLF

I USED TO LOVE THE ZOO until I could see how terrifying it was for a wild animal to be introduced to things he had never seen or heard before. All Romy knew was the forest. Imagine how high he jumped when my mom used the blender for the first time or my dad turned on the TV. Even with such obstacles, my mom was soon amazed at how Romy behaved with me. He followed me endlessly.

"Everett, look." She pointed to Romy walking in front of me as I headed down the stairs. "It's like he's making sure to be there if she falls."

"I'm telling you, Amelia, he was protecting her in that cave. Never seen noth'n' like it."

My mother learned the error of her ways when she bought regular dog food for a wolf. I would sit next to his bowl, trying to get him to eat, but he would refuse, putting his snout in the air. "Mommy, Romy thinks this food is stinky."

When my dad came home from work, he looked at the bowl and laughed. "Amelia, you're trying to give a *wolf* Kibbles and Bits?"

Maybe every little girl sees her daddy this way, but my father seemed larger than life, stronger than an ox, and completely in love with my mother, the tiny homemaker with country grit and a bite that left marks if needed.

She stood in her apron with her hands on her hips. "Well, what the hell am I supposed to do, Everett? Go shoot a deer for him?"

My father thought about it then opened the back door. "Romy, go get your dinner." My mother and I watched Romy run out the door and into the woods. My father shut the door and shrugged. "Let the wolf be a wolf."

They were words he would come to repeat quite often.

I was so worried that night, waiting by the back door for my Romy.

I didn't know if he'd ever hunted on his own before. *Does he know how? Will he starve? Will he get lost? Will something eat him?* But I had nothing to worry about, because when I stood on the back porch and called out to him, a distant howl was his way of telling me he was fine.

Later that night, as soon as my wolf came running to the back door, I opened it, and he sprinted into my open arms. "He's home! Romy made it home!"

My father was on our old couch, watching TV. "See? Let the wolf be a wolf."

"Oh, *Daddy*. His belly feels *bigger*." I touched and examined the protruding stomach.

"Good, Romy. Ya just saved me some cash." He looked at my mom, who snuggled next to him. "Could you imagine how expensive it would have been to feed him as he grows?"

"Grows?" My mother went pale.

"Romy was still with his mother. He has to be a pup."

My mother stared at Romy sitting quietly while I continued to poke and prod his distended belly. "How much bigger, Everett? He's already got to be eighty pounds. He doubles Marlena's size and weight."

And he always would. As I grew, he grew.

That night, I insisted Romy take a bath with me in our upstairs bathroom. My father came up to check on me and froze when he saw bubbles sticking to gray, matted fur and a tiara on Romy's soaked head. "He's a princess, Daddy."

My father shook his head and walked to the stairs, mumbling, "Poor guy. Let the wolf be a wolf."

The next morning, I woke to delightful licks from my furry friend. My mother was putting clothes in my drawers. She scrunched her face. "Oh, Marlena, that's horrible." She liked her home clean *and* her child free of germs.

I just smiled through the tongue swipes. "Mommy, Romy's just giving kisses."

Romy adjusted so well to his new environment that I thought it was time to play. My father sat on the dilapidated couch, trying to relax after work, when a blur ran in front of the TV. Then I ran past, hot on the blur's trail. "Romy! I said, put this dress on!"

My father would go back to his old TV with an antenna on top, saying, "Poor guy. Let the wolf be a wolf."

When I pulled out sparkly makeup, somehow my father thought it was dinner time and opened the back door. The traitor, Romy, ran outside, minus the lipstick I was trying to apply. My father shut the door, mumbling, "Let a wolf..." as he sat back down. I opened the door and hollered for Romy then stood at that back door, tapping my angry foot. Again, his far-off-in-the-distance howl told me he was fine being a wolf.

Once, Romy brought home *his* dinner while my mother cooked *us* dinner. I opened the back door, and in came Romy, dragging a stinky, leftover coyote carcass. Romy proudly laid his catch—or steal—next to his bowl. I think he wanted to be more like us.

My father glanced over from the couch and whispered, "Oh shit."

My mother turned from the stove and screamed.

And she kept screaming.

"Everett! There is blood all over my floors. I JUST MOPPED!"

My father dragged out the dead, bloody animal. I was sure both he *and* Romy had their tails between their legs. My father whispered, "Romy! We're buds! Ya trying to get me killed?"

Romy lowered his head, following him out the door. I guessed that was his apology.

The new school year started, and Romy and I had a very hard time separating, or I should say, my mother had a very hard time separating us. The first day, she dragged me kicking and screaming to the bus stop, which was our front yard, with a whining wolf in tow. When I got on the bus, it was already full with no empty rows, just empty spots next to students, who, for some reason, did not want the snotty-nosed brat who just caused a scene at the bus stop to sit next to them. I was about to turn and high-tail it right back off the bus when I heard a boy ask, "Is that your wolf?"

He had short blond hair. I sniffled and nodded, not willing to elaborate.

"Cool." He moved over for me to sit next to him. Reluctantly, I took the seat because through the bus window, I could see my mother waving her finger at me. Her stern look told me to sit, or I was gonna get a spanking. I decided the blond-haired boy couldn't be worse than a sore hiney.

"I'm T. Well, Trevor, but T for short. That's Jimmy." He pointed to a little boy with orange hair, sitting in the row in front of him. "We call Jimmy Hound 'cause his daddy says he's the best tracker there is." I couldn't understand why Jimmy wasn't just called Jimmy. It was what his mommy'd named him. And T? That made no sense either. I was going to call him Trevor.

Jimmy/Hound—who could barely see over the back of his seat with his pretty green eyes—waved to me. "You want to go hunt'n' with us?"

I didn't wave back, nor did I answer.

T/Trevor asked me, "What's your name?"

That was when I saw Trevor's chocolate-brown eyes, and since I loved chocolate, I shyly answered, "Marlena."

"Nice to meet you, Marlena. Hound and me are in first grade. What grade are you?"

"Umm, kindergarten?"

"Oh," was all he said.

That concerned me. "Oh?"

Trevor took a deep breath. "The big K can be rough, especially for someone as puny as your—"

As my 'puny' arms crossed my 'puny' chest, my angry face told Trevor I might be little, but I bit. I tried tapping my angry foot for emphasis, but my legs were too short, and it couldn't reach the floor of the bus. So my angry foot stayed mid-swing in the air, flapping around aimlessly.

Trevor laughed, putting his palms up in surrender. "Whoa! Never mind. I see you can handle yourself." He looked out the window as we drove down the dirt road. "No wonder that wolf likes you."

That comment made me stop and think because our friendship— Romy's and mine—came so naturally I'd never given a thought as to why or how. Did he like me because I was a handful? Because I was one of the only humans he knew? Then I got to thinking about Romy's secret—now my secret too—and I knew I'd never tell anyone at school about it.

If Mother Wolf was part human, I assumed chances were high that Romy was too, and she had asked me to help him. I decided that everything I learned at school would be Romy's lessons at night. And that is exactly what I did. My father would just shake his head when I pointed to a book and made Romy focus. My mother would hush my father, saying it was good for me to reinforce what I was learning.

The school schedule ended up working out the way my mom had

16

promised. At school, I had my human friends, Trevor and Jimmy, and at home, I had my furry one, Romy. Trevor and Jimmy were a grade above me, so I only got to see them during recess and at lunchtime, but I liked them. They accepted me, unlike the girls in my class. I was a tad tomboyish for their liking.

I quickly learned T was captain of the monkey bars, and Jimmy was co-captain. I appreciated their need to lead and admired them for that. This somehow caused me to become the third wheel, and the duo became a solid trio. Trevor took a special liking to me, so no one dared mess with me on the playground. Unbeknownst to me, I found this attractive, and began to grow a crush on the alpha named T.

Lunchtime was when and where I shared my food with Trevor because when Trevor and Jimmy would come over to play, and Trevor wanted some of the snack my mom made us, a growl would quickly remind Trevor who the *true* alpha of my backyard was. *Romy.*

I would shrug to Trevor and give what food I didn't want to my wolf.

Other than that, Trevor and Romy were fine together. Trevor, Jimmy, Romy, and I would run through the woods, playing hide and seek or any other game *I* could think of. I was a little bossy, and in T and Hound style, they appreciated it.

I was told how, one night, my mom woke to a wet nose nudging her. "Go lay down, Romy. I'm sleeping." She said Romy was persistent and gave another snout nudge. She whispered loudly, "Stop it!"

My father later said that was when he woke, asking, "What's wrong?"

"Damn wolf wants to chitchat or something." She rolled away from Romy and into my father.

He closed his eyes and mumbled, "Weird, he never leaves that kid's side."

They both froze.

When they quickly sat up and saw Romy nervously pacing in their bedroom doorway, they scrambled out of bed and ran up the stairs, following an agitated wolf, to find me in bed with an extremely high fever.

I cried it wasn't bath time as my parents struggled to put my overheated body into a tub of cool water. My mom was on her knees with my father standing over her, both trying to catch my limbs that rebelled against their efforts to immerse me. I was too young to understand their terrified, worried faces.

What stopped my repeated escape attempts was Romy stepping around my parents and joining me in the tub of tidal waves I had caused. He sat in front of me and gave me a big lick across my angry, snotty face.

I sniffled as I clung to my wolf, but I stayed in the tub.

My mother's tension stopped knotting her brow. Her long blond hair was not tightly wound in its usual bun. I watched as her blue eyes, the ones my father said I shared, tear while she calmly kept pouring a cup of bath water over my shoulders. I was going to ask her why she was about to cry, but she quietly said, "Everett?"

My father, exhaling in relief, massaged her tense shoulders. "Yeah?" His black hair and beard were speckled with gray.

A timid voice I had not heard my mother use said, "Romy is allowed to bring dead animals into this house if he wants to." She began to cry. "This damn hairy mutt can do whatever he wants, whenever he wants. Okay? Everett, do you hear me? Okay?"

I shivered in the water, watching my rugged father look adoringly at my mother. He kissed the top of her head. "Okay."

My parents weren't model-beautiful. They were possibly even plain, but their hearts showed me the most important kind of beauty.

The years passed, and my crush on Trevor grew as my memory of what Romy could possibly be faded. Visits to his mother's gravesite slowly diminished, and my youth caused her memory to fade also. Romy had become a wonderful, unlikely pet from the wild with which I'd built a special, one-of-a-kind relationship. Trevor became the young man I would marry someday.

Trevor, Jimmy, and I were friends who had a lot of firsts together: first movie at a movie theater, first roller-skating night, first egging of a house, first beer. Most of the time, we had a hairy sidekick, unless we went somewhere other than my house or the woods.

I thought it was because of his intimidating size that my parents never took Romy anywhere, but my father had once told me it was illegal to have this kind of pet. When I'd looked worried, he'd stated, "What they don't know won't hurt them, little girl. Right?"

I wasn't sure about my father's logic, but I *was* sure I wanted Romy kept out of harm's way. My father had shrugged. "If someone were to ask questions, I'll say that it's not my fault a wolf hangs around here sometimes."

In fact, there were no issues with Romy until I was fifteen.

Trevor and Jimmy were growing into young men with growing *interest*. Jimmy was no longer an awkward carrot top but a handsome green-eyed guy who could hold his own against T. Girls adored him and his sense of humor. When Trevor and Jimmy went off to high school, they were a pair of hormones on a mission, and I was left to a year without them in middle school. That was when I realized how *our* friends were truly T and Hound's friends. Trevor and Jimmy were more popular, and I was more reclusive. I just didn't feel comfortable with anyone but them.

Not seeing them as much because they were chasing girls stung, and I called off the wedding Trevor was not aware he was involved in. On the back porch, I hugged Romy and informed him that he was now going to have to marry me. His tongue left a trail of slobber across my face, telling me he was much obliged.

Things changed when I became a freshman in high school. Jimmy was so excited. He kept telling me, "We got our girl back! The trio is a trio again! Love you, Mar-cakes."

But Trevor? He was standoffish. I would try to talk to him, which wasn't easy with all the girls fighting for his attention, but Trevor was always paying attention to the guys around me.

"Trevor! Why are you being distant?" I pinched the bridge of my nose. I was so frustrated I could've spit nails right there in the school hallway.

He didn't answer or even glance at me, just scowled at someone behind me. "What are you looking at?"

Peering over my shoulder, I saw a guy walking past me with his hands in the air. "Nothing, T. I know she's off limits."

Apparently, guys were becoming interested in me, and this was not sitting well with Big T. I faced Trevor, tapping my toes. "What do you care? You have girls all over you."

The muscles in Trevor's neck appeared strained. "Stop looking at me with those blues, Marlena."

Jimmy chuckled while digging in his locker.

Trevor growled. "Shut it, Hound."

He shut his locker door, laughing. "Oh, you're just pissed because our girl here has changed over the past year." He pointed to Trevor. "Choose or lose, my friend."

"Not asking for your opinion." Trevor's jaw was as strained as his neck.

I leaned against a locker and huffed. "Jimmy, what are you talking about?"

Jimmy seemed extremely entertained with whatever was transpiring. He said to himself, "Let's see. She needs an example." He scoured the hallway, running his fingers through his red hair. Finding what he wanted, he lifted his chin. "Yo, Scott!"

Scott walked past us. He replied with a chin lift of his own.

"Marlena is looking for a movie date Friday night. You in?"

Scott's feet became concreted to the flooring, causing a fellow student to collide with his back. My jaw unhinged itself as I stumbled forward to stop Jimmy, but I only stuttered, not forming any words in the English language. Jimmy winked. "Don't worry, girl. I got your back." He focused on Scott again. "So, you in?"

Scott's eyes lit up, and he took a step toward me. "Yeah, I'm in."

Before I could explain that Jimmy had lost his ever-loving mind, Trevor pulled my back to his chest, wrapped his arm firmly around my waist, and spoke over the top of my head to Scott. "You're not in nothin' of hers. Hound's an asshole, and Marlena's mine."

Jimmy stepped into my stunned view and grinned in my face. "Understand now?" He put his arm around Scott's shoulder, walking him away. "Sorry, dude. Had to prove a point."

My cheeks blushed with hope. *Could this be?* I slowly turned to face Trevor, who still had his arm around me, holding my body up against his. I inhaled, nervous he didn't mean those words. Trevor refused to look at me while he cleared his throat. "I guess I should've, uh, asked if you wanted this but... Jimmy told me you had a crush on me... I... I just couldn't... handle the thought... of you crush'n' on anyone else."

I exhaled.

Music. To. My. Ears.

"Okay, Trevor. I won't like anyone but you."

Brown eyes finally looked down to me. The strain left Trevor's neck as he moved my blond hair from my face. "So... you and me?"

It wasn't romance out of a movie, but it was coming from Trevor, which made it great.

"Yeah." I felt my eyelashes bat of their own accord. "You and me."

Trevor had officially become my boyfriend.

The other male in my life had been eating like a pig, rather than a wolf, and was packing on weight at an alarming rate. My mom worried because a wolf should have been done growing years ago. I was scrawny but still managed to reach the height of five foot six. Romy on all fours was above my bony hip, the height of a Great Dane, but with the girth of a Rottweiler on steroids, weighing in at one hundred and seventy-something pounds.

It was hard to know exactly because to weigh him we had to subtract my father's weight from the total. Only problem was, Romy seemed to prefer his paws on the ground. My father would have to try to hold a massive, moving wolf while standing on my mom's overwhelmed bathroom scale. My father being a strong man due to his manual labor job was the only reason this was even possible.

Either way, a few weeks after Trevor and I became an item, my little bed squeaked its protest. I grumbled about long, furry limbs taking up the whole mattress as I arranged my blankets over me, getting ready for bed. The hall light lit my dark room while my father and mother stood in my doorway.

My dad said, "He's just gonna have to start sleeping on the floor."

My jaw dropped at such a horrid suggestion. Romy painfully howled his complaint. My father laughed as he walked away, talking to himself. "I swear he understands the human language. He practically knows algebra with how she schools him every day. Shouldn't the wolf *act* like a wolf?" I might have forgotten Romy's mother's words, but teaching Romy was habit and had continued through the years.

My mother stayed at my doorway, shadowing my room. "Marlena, he's just too big and getting bigger!"

The overgrown wolf was now in my lap, whimpering. The bed squeaked its own cries. "Mom, *please*! I've had him with me since I was—"

"Six years old. I know, I know." She sighed. "I'm just concerned that your dad has been right all along. We should let him be—well, a wolf."

At that point, the big ol' bad wolf taking refuge in my lap put his face under his paws to hide.

At sixteen, serious issues with Romy began to show themselves. It was no longer simple problems like him being too big for my bed. Anyone involved with Romy and me was starting to feel the pressure and responsibility of our unique relationship. If Trevor tried to hold me in his lap or showed too much affection toward me, a low rumble would escape from Romy.

Jimmy would laugh in pure amusement, as usual, while Trevor argued with my wolf. "Knock it off, Romy. We have to share!"

When I was a sophomore and Trevor a junior, we became a more serious couple. When Jimmy wasn't with us, Trevor and I would sneak off to kiss in the woods, but were always found and interrupted by Romy, who had now packed on *another* twenty pounds, weighing in at one hundred and ninety-something. My mother's scale was almost maxed out.

"Marlena, I can't ever get you alone!" Trevor loudly complained as Romy nudged his way in between us.

Leaning back against the tree, I playfully said, "That's the way my daddy likes it, Trevor." I petted the wolf now sitting proudly between my legs.

Lusty brown eyes smiled at me, just like his lips did. "Why don't you ever call me T?"

"Because that's not what your mama named you, and it feeds your inflated ego."

Trevor threw his head backward as he laughed. "My inflated ego?" He turned on what he considered his animal magnetism. "I'll have you know that I'm constantly approached with offers from other girls…"

Romy snorted then rubbed the top of his huge head all over my belly while I ruffled the fur under his chin. The soft fur felt the way I imagined clouds felt like—*oops, wasn't Trevor saying something?*

"… promising me a *really* good time, but with you, I barely get to cop a feel with this"—Trevor gestured to my favorite creature on earth —"furry, overgrown monstrosity *you* call a pet."

Yes, that comment won T a warning growl from Romy.

"Easy, Cujo," Trevor said with attitude, not fear.

Trevor wasn't the only one with concerns. One day when I got off the bus after school, I was surprised to see my father already home from work.

"Why home so early?" I rocked back and forth, trying to stay on my feet while Romy obsessively rubbed and rubbed the full length of his body all over me.

My father had yet to answer me, seeming distracted watching Romy. He pointed to me and asked my mother, "Is this what you're talking about?"

Just then, Romy stuck his nose in my butt. I pushed his snout away, annoyed—as I was usually was—when dealing with the unnecessary intrusion. "Romy! Knock it off."

Mom stood there, her apron showing smears of her labor, and blew out a deep breath. "Yes, every day lately."

I petted the top of Romy's head, still wobbling from his heavy weight pushing on me as he circled my legs and hips, and I shrugged. "So I look like a hair factory by the time he's done. All dogs like butts. What's the big deal?"

My father didn't answer me till that night when we sat on the top step of our back porch. There was a nice breeze carrying the scent of the woods. He drank his evening beer while we both watched my poor Romy become more and more territorial, urinating all over the perimeter of our property. The moon shone down on our growing issue.

"It's normal, I guess," my father told me, "but he should be out in his natural surroundings, not a domestic environment… and possibly not all over my little girl. His attachment to you is becoming, well, a bit unnerving."

I thought that was absurd. "So he likes sniffing butts."

"Only yours, little girl."

I winced. "What do you want me to do, Dad? Have him neutered?"

His shoulders bounced with his chuckle. "No, my buddy might bite me after that, and that may cause Romy to personally neuter your boyfriend." He took a worried breath. "I'm just saying maybe… the time for… him to—" He stopped in midthought then said with heart, "Just keep your mind open. He's changing, little girl." My father patted my shoulder, got up, and went inside to my mother, who was cooking dinner.

I stayed and watched my best friend as he became more and more agitated, running from one corner of our large yard to the other as if chasing

23

invisible beings he felt he needed to piss on, his massive back paws kicking dirt behind him like a proud rooster.

As Romy strutted—no, prowled—through the trees at the edge of my property, I had a vision of a darker wolf doing the same prowl. I figured my mind was playing tricks on me as the thoughts became more like memories.

An extremely dark wolf that was as tall as I, as a little girl...

A female wolf who would watch me as I played...

They protected my chocolate castle.

It felt as if my head was going to explode as memories invaded my brain. I lay back on the porch to close my eyes and try to clear my head, to let the cool wood calm me.

One day, the two wolves brought a baby gray wolf.

The mother wolf dying and transforming into a human...

I sat up in a hurry, bending over, grabbing my head as more memories assaulted me.

Romy howling out his cries to the moon...

Mother Wolf in wolf form again...

I hid my face in my hands, trying to trust a little girl's memories that seemed so damn real. "This can't be," I told myself, but deep down, I knew the memories were true.

Franticly, I scanned my yard for Romy, the need to protect him once again rising. He wasn't there. I called out his name and heard his distant howl answering me.

Waiting for Romy's return, I gasped when I saw dark, proud Father Wolf walking toward me, coming out of the nighttime forest. For a moment, I believed Romy's father had returned until I realized I was not looking at Romy's father. I was seeing Romy now *resembling* his father. No longer was I seeing Romy as the sweet, overgrown wolf I believed him to be. Now, I saw the mature Romy, whose presence alone demanded respect.

He's changing, little girl. My father's words echoed through my mind.

"Oh, dear God, help me," I whispered in fear for my friend.

Romy must have heard me or sensed my emotional state because his huge paws dug into the dirt for traction. He gained speed and rushed to me. Tears quietly fell from my eyes at the shock I was experiencing. I reached for his face with both my shaky hands as he slid to a stop. "Can you *truly* understand me?"

He let out a whimper while staring deep into my eyes.

"I'm either madder than the Mad Hatter or—" I stared at him for another moment. "If you can truly understand me, bark twice for the answer yes. If I'm nuts, well, bark once?"

Two barks rang in my ears.

Chapter Four

Folklore and the Kissing Tree

EVERYTHING BECAME COMPLICATED AFTER THAT. Everything seemed so... magnetized. Up 'til that point, I had been sure of myself and, yes, bossy at times, but now, I was so worried for my friend that the selfishness I had owned proudly was dissipating. I viewed Romy completely differently. My bed was now *our* bed. My room was now *our* room. And the thought of him eating out of a bowl or chasing his dinner through the woods concerned me with how it would affect him after his possible change.

I wondered who would Romy be if not Romy anymore? And if my mind wasn't wondering enough, my parents and I sat down to watch a movie about an alien. The story was not related to my wolf, so I was happy for the distraction. But the distraction only upped my worry to a whole new level. This poor creature ended up stranded on earth with none of his family. He managed to take on the human form to blend, but once someone found out his secret, the government stepped in and forcefully took him to a top-secret lab. The alien was tortured from one brutal science project to the next. It was merciless in the name of science. It was cruel.

Once his mutilated body finally succumbed to the violence, his leftover parts were sold to other countries and rich experimental laboratories. My eyes slowly glanced to see my wolf studying the TV. His shivers told me he understood what his possible change could bring him. Terrified gray eyes met mine.

"What is with you lately?" Trevor asked, pulling me from memories of the previous night.

Standing in the cafeteria line, I blinked. "Uh, nothing… why?"

"Because talking to you is like trying to communicate with outer space lately."

I shivered, thinking of the tragic alien.

If only I could tell Trevor and Jimmy and have someone by my side to help Romy… But seeing everything with new eyes also helped me see what Trevor had become again: T, egotistical ruler of the playground. The playground had just morphed into high school. And I got to see what Trevor saw, a girl smiling at him with a not-so-hidden message. I dared a glance to Jimmy for a silent confirmation. Jimmy frowned before shamefully looking away. *If my being somewhat distracted is enough to lose Trevor's interest so quickly, how can I trust him with my most precious secret?*

I couldn't. So I didn't.

And telling Jimmy was pretty much telling Trevor, so he wasn't an option either.

Like every day, Romy waited for me to get home from school, sitting in my front yard as if I were still six. As the bus stopped, Trevor looked out his window and sneered. "Shocker. The mutt awaits its faithful owner." I got up, ignoring his thoughtless remark, but froze when under his breath, Trevor said, "Shouldn't he be dead by now?"

I had read that a wolf's life expectancy in the wild was between six and ten years. In captivity, they could live up to eighteen years. I didn't know which to consider Romy, since he had much freedom. I undeniably dreaded the day of his passing.

After all my worrying about what Romy might be, hearing *those* words spoken out loud shot an electrical current through my heart. Jimmy, who still sat in front of Trevor and me every day, warned, "T!"

Trevor took one look at me and jumped out of his seat. "Oh, God, babe, I'm so sorry. I didn't mean that, and you know it." He grabbed me and kissed my head over and over. "I'm sorry."

I silently nodded without returning the kisses and exited the bus.

At the dinner table, Mom and Dad ate their chili. Sounds of spoons clanking against bowls made my insides ache. Every noise agitated me. Even the smell of the best chili in the world now brought me discomfort.

"Why so quiet, Marlena?"

I looked away from the full spoon I'd been staring at. "Tired, I guess."

A big snout came to rest in my lap.

My father didn't approve. "Romy, not at the table. Go lie down."

My dad speaking to a being who might become human someday as if he were simply an unaware dog made my skin hurt. Romy, of course, retreated—obeyed—and *that* made me incredibly irritable. "Dad, please don't. I know you have rules but I… I need him right now."

My dad tilted his head, clearly perplexed.

Romy waited quietly for further instructions. That made my stomach queasy. I didn't want Romy to need permission to react.

Luckily, my father loved me and gestured to Romy. My wolf stepped forward and laid his head back in my lap. That sweet, simple action made something inside me break. I began to cry.

My dad touched my shoulder. "He's with you, little girl. What's wrong?"

Tears kept falling. "I-I'm not sure. May I please be excused?"

My stunned parents didn't move or blink their eyes. I'd never cared if I needed permission nor asked for it. I did as I chose. But seeing Romy being treated this way, I felt it was only right that I also have rules.

Father was speechless, so my mom stuttered, "U-Uh, yes. You're, uh, excused."

I barely voiced a thank you and went upstairs. My wolf followed.

My body collapsed to my bed and refused to move. Every muscle felt drained of energy. The bed creaked before I felt a wet nose under my chin. I forced my tired arm around him and hugged my wolf, searching and finding comfort. "Romy?"

Two barks.

"I need to do my homework." I was more than fatigued. I had no drive to accomplish my task. Romy immediately leapt from my bed and dragged my backpack to the bed. I weakly smiled. "But I also need a ten-minute nap." Romy glanced at my digital clock. Red numbers said *6:45.*

My eyes closed.

A lick to my face woke me from the coma I'd drifted into. "Romy, I'm too tired. More sleep."

One bark.

I huffed and puffed but opened my eyes. Red numbers next to my bed read *6:55*. I peered at the wolf waiting for me to get up. "I'm not crazy, am I?"

One bark.

With encouragement from Romy, I finally smiled with some energy. "Okay then, homework time it is."

Sitting at my desk as I did every night, I noticed something I'd taken for granted: a wolf planted next to me. With the old memories resurfacing, I paid more attention to Romy studying what I did on my computer. "You're still learning every day, aren't you?"

Two barks.

Thinking about all the schoolwork I'd done in front of him, all the books I'd read and the TV shows I'd watched, I realized Romy wouldn't be behind when or if he changed his form.

I stared at my computer and couldn't believe I had not thought of this before. "Want to search Google for your possible ancestors?"

The windows rattled with his two enthusiastic barks.

"Marlena?" My mom called from downstairs.

"We're okay. He just got excited."

"Amelia, he was so damn loud I spilled my beer."

"Does that mean you need another, Everett?"

"You're so good to me."

Romy and I searched and searched the Internet. The one thing every site agreed on was… "Well, Romy, you don't exist."

Two barks.

I laughed, petting his head. "I know. You sure do exist."

We learned that Romy's mother and father were possibly a part of what people believed to be folklore, a werewolf. My research found some terminology of the different names for werewolves coming from Ancient Greece. If what was thought to be folklore actually existed, I learned Romy's family tree might have *very* deep roots.

Some considered werewolves' beginnings to be a berserker in the ninth century. The man wasn't *transforming* into a wolf but had great strength, and it was said he acted like one.

"Maybe that's where it all began?"

No bark. Romy didn't know either.

Somehow, reading about witches and lycanthropes and how some people were charged with witchery and lycanthropy made me feel less crazy, especially since there were examples of these cases up until the mid-1800s. "Maybe werewolves have learned how to stay under the radar since then."

No bark.

"Okay, my furry friend. Apparently, you are a loup-garou, and according to Hollywood and many major and minor film productions, you can start your own pack if ya bite people." I felt so much affection for my friend as I petted him. "Can you imagine me a wolf?"

One bark.

"Me either, handsome. Let's get some shut-eye."

My seventeenth birthday came and went. Trevor had taken me to the movies. I questioned his choice of sitting in the back row until I had to keep pushing his hands from my chest. "What are you doing?"

He kissed my neck. "Being a teenager? Maybe you should try being one, too."

I didn't understand how allowing him to touch my breasts meant I was appropriately acting like a teenager. My heart pounded, feeling pressured into an activity that felt rushed. I became rigid in my movie seat as Trevor gently caressed me.

His hand paused. "Did you stop breathing?"

I had. "Sorry."

Trevor blew out air as he sat back in his chair. "Whatever."

When it came to Romy, I had relaxed again. We'd found our old groove, only now I had much more respect for his needs and wants. My junior year had come, and with the beginning of a new school year, Trevor and I were finding our end. At the Kissing Tree, better known as the Let-Me-Try-And-Touch-You-As-Fast-As-I-Can-Before-Your-Mutt-Finds-Us Tree, Trevor had finally had enough.

"What do you mean, you don't understand?" Trevor almost yelled at me. "If I try to kiss you right now, *he*"—Trevor pointed to the wolf, once again sitting between my legs as I leaned back against the tree—"won't let me!"

I knew the end was coming, but I'd been with Trevor for all my school life, except for one year, and that year had been hard on me. Saying goodbye to Trevor was saying hello to loneliness. And I feared that if Trevor and I broke up, I would lose Jimmy, too. Not wanting to lose my buddies—my only human friends—I sank to a low point I never wished to sink to again.

"Romy, go home."

Instantly, Romy's body jolted between my legs, as if I had jolted his heart. He slowly got up and walked a couple of steps toward home. He turned back to me with eyes that were... hurt.

Looking away from my friend, I gestured toward our house. "Go home, Romy."

Romy did, with his head and tail hanging low.

Facing me, Trevor's head cocked to the side with a questioning glare. My shame made me look away from him, too. My breathing became labored. Pain invaded my heart. I stayed leaning against the tree so my suddenly weak body could withstand the misery. I was completely torn between a *need* and a *want*. I wanted Trevor because, well, I didn't know how to do school without him. But that *want* was not what was causing the unbearable ache in my chest. That was my *need*, an incredible pull for Romy and something lurking within him.

A finger gently raised my chin I hadn't realized had fallen. "There will always be three in this relationship."

I looked at Trevor, feeling remorseful, but there was no denying it any longer, not even to myself. Romy came first. *Always had... always will.*

Trevor could've yelled and screamed during our breakup, but he didn't. He took a deep breath and quietly left me standing at the Kissing Tree, wondering if I'd ever be kissed again.

That night, Romy didn't respond to my questions or comments. He just lay in my bed, watching me with very little movement. If I hadn't betrayed him, I would've sworn he was sick, but Romy never got sick. I didn't bother telling him Trevor and I were over. I was simply too tired and a tad bit brokenhearted. I had planned to marry the Big T from the playground, but life sometimes has its own plans, and mine were in the shape of a wolf.

Getting on the bus the next morning caused a wave of acid to build in my stomach. I had sat next to Trevor every day for almost eleven years, and now there was a new girl. Trevor wouldn't even look at me. I stood there, dumbfounded, swallowing a lump in my throat.

"Hey." Jimmy opened his arms.

My knees almost buckled as I rushed to him. I sat next to Jimmy for the first time and fell into his waiting chest. Relief exuded from my body as I realized I hadn't lost Jimmy in the divorce.

"What are you doing?" Trevor asked from behind us.

Jimmy held me tightly. "Being a friend to *our* friend, you moron. Just because you feel the need to morph into a male slut overnight doesn't mean Mar-cakes deserves to be alone while she's forced to witness it."

"Piss off, Hound," Trevor muttered.

"Whatever, T. When you get through this phase, you'll be thankful I was here for her."

Trevor went quiet. Then I heard him quietly say, "Carrie, do you mind giving me some space this morning? I need to think. Catch ya at lunch?"

"Sure, T." I heard wet lips connecting. "That's for last night."

I buried myself deeper into Jimmy's embrace.

Carrie went and sat with a giggling girlfriend while my heart and ego took a horrendous blow. Jimmy spoke over my head as I hid in embarrassment. "Jesus, T."

Trevor leaned forward. "I. Did. Not. Cheat."

Jimmy's voice rumbled in the chest I wouldn't let go of. "Nor did you let a huge breakup settle before getting your—"

I begged, "Shhh. Please don't say it." I didn't want a visual of what Trevor and his private parts did hours after we called it quits. "And please don't fight because of me." I sat up, my red eyes finding Trevor. "You're right. You didn't cheat on me." I looked between Jimmy and Trevor. "*Please*, both of you drop this... I'm feeling a-a little sick."

After staring at me for a moment, Trevor slammed his body back and elbowed his seat. Hard.

At school, the rumor mill was in full force, and Trevor's status elevated. The lunch line was embarrassingly lonely until Jimmy cut in and joined me. "Stand tall, beautiful. Those bitches crawling up his ass ain't got noth'n' on you."

I tried to force back my hunched shoulders, feeling pathetic. "Wanna eat lunch with this loner?"

"Whatcha think I'm stand'n' here for? To be your eye candy?"

I actually giggled. "My eye candy?"

Jimmy saw my smile and matched it. "Some find redheads hot."

I grabbed my tray. "I'm one of them. And I'm a sucker for dreamy green eyes."

"Keep stroking my ego. I like it," Jimmy teased as he heavily loaded his tray.

Walking past my old lunch table was uncomfortable, to say the least. My seat was taken, and Trevor smiled through new affections until he saw Jimmy and me pass by him. I didn't want to be the cause of a rift between T and Hound. "Jimmy, you don't have to do this."

He found us an empty table. "T's being his hormones' little bitch—not his finest moment." We both sat down. "But as you know, there's a good guy under the layers of females presently all over him. And he *will* regret this—when he sees straight again."

Just then, a chair slid from the table as a tray was set down to my right. Trevor sat with heavy shoulders. "I owe you both an apology, Marlena. You and I have far too much history for me to have done that to you. Hound, you're right. I should've waited before I—"

I put my hand up. "Please don't say it. Picturing you naked with—just please stop."

Trevor gave out a lengthy exhale. "I'm such an asshole."

"Yep," Jimmy quickly agreed as he took a bite of questionable food.

"You're not helping, Hound," Trevor complained.

Jimmy casually opened his milk. "You're here doing right, aren't ya?"

He was. Trevor was sitting next to me, manning up.

"Thank you for that," I whispered to Trevor. "Thank you for trying to mend me."

Another quiet moment passed. Trevor asked me, "Friends?"

The word *friend* hit me directly in the chest, but not for the reasons I expected. It was because he was more than a boyfriend to me. I loved him because he *was* my friend. I nodded and choked out, "I need you," through the emotions that owned me.

"Oh, girl." He pulled me to him. "I need you, too. I'm so sorry for hurting you like this." Still holding me, he said to Jimmy, "Thank you." My hand reached behind me. Jimmy acknowledged my silent gratitude, accepting my hand.

Riding the school bus home, I was amazed by how so much could transpire in less than twenty-four hours. I was now single but happily friends with my ex, appreciating Jimmy even more, and about to take a leap into my new world.

As the bus pulled up to my house, I was grabbing my bag off the floor when Jimmy said, "Oh, shit."

Not yet looking at my new bus partner, I asked, "What?" But when I did, I saw deep-rooted fear. Jimmy was frozen, rooted to the bus seat. Then, he said words that rocked me to the core—the core of my foundation, my reason for existence. "*No Romy.*"

Terror shot through me. For the very first time, Romy was not waiting for me.

Knowing that no matter how mad he was, Romy would never abandon me, I jumped out of my seat and raced to the exit with Jimmy on my heels. Trevor followed us down the aisle. "I'm coming, Marlena!"

I ran off the bus. "Something's wrong!"

"I know, girl. We'll find him." Trevor tried to assure me, but he didn't sound convinced.

Bursting through my front door, I ran past my parents' bedroom and the stairs, screaming, "Romy!"

Mom came rushing out of the kitchen, wiping her hands with a towel. "He's not out front?"

"No!"

"He hasn't barked to come in all day." My mom opened the back door. She sang out, "Romy."

We all went quiet and still and waited to hear his answering howl.

There wasn't one.

I catapulted my body up the stairs, searching. My bedroom was empty. "He's not here! Mom! Trevor! He's not here!" I came running back down and tripped, crashing to the bottom step and into a waiting Trevor.

He checked me for injuries. Finding none, he grabbed my shoulders. "Listen to me. We *will* find him, but if you kill yourself beforehand—"

"You're right." I nodded frantically. "You're right, but I should've known something was wrong. He was upset last night. I just thought he was mad at me."

"Marlena!" Trevor tried to get me to focus. "Where do we search first?"

"Umm… umm." I was trying to think of his favorite spot, but he was a wolf! He would run for miles at a time. "*All* over the woods." My body shook with adrenaline.

Trevor's forehead touched mine. "Okay then, that's what we'll do. Search *all* of the woods with our personal hound."

My eyes closed as I thanked God for Trevor and Jimmy. Trevor might have dumped me, but he cared too much to let me suffer alone.

"I won't sleep 'til he's found." Jimmy headed to the back door.

"I'll call Everett." Mom was already reaching for the phone hanging on the kitchen wall. She talked into the phone as Trevor, Jimmy, and I ran out the back door to find my wolf.

Standing in the backyard, Trevor and I called for Romy while Hound walked around, trying to make sense of the many wolf prints Romy had left behind. Trevor and I waited for the answering howl we desperately needed.

Nothing.

Trevor yelled in frustration, "Damn it, Romy! Answer me now!"

My ears tingled because I was listening *so hard*.

Nothing.

We knew a wolf could hear us from miles away. No howl either meant he was too far to hear us—which had never happened before—or he *couldn't* answer us. I grabbed my stomach. "Oh, Trevor—"

"I got a fresh trail," Jimmy interrupted me from the edge of the property.

The three of us headed into the woods, rushing, letting branches scratch our faces and bodies.

The sun was setting when I heard, "Anything?" My father had caught up to us. I dove into his arms for the comfort only a daddy can offer. Arms wrapped around me. "My little girl, breathe."

I was so nervous I couldn't speak, so Trevor answered for me. "Nothing and no howls."

Jimmy was on one knee, looking at the fallen leaves as if they were talking to him. "His weight distribution is changing here... like a drunk wolf." He stood again and kept walking. We followed as my imagination went wild with all that could have happened to Romy. The sun was going down, along with my spirits. Jimmy reassured me as he searched the ground. "I will find him, Mar-cakes."

I blew out a shaky breath, trying not to lose hope.

"Wait!" Jimmy put his hands out to stop us from walking across the earth speaking to him. When we did, he looked intently at the ground, turning in place.

I pleaded, "What is it?"

"Hold on." He took a couple of tentative steps. "I think he fell." Jimmy got on his hands and knees, pointing. "He pulled himself with his front paws." He crawled to some thick shrubbery. After looking in, Jimmy yelled, "He's here!"

I don't know if I ran, crawled, or flew, but I was half in the bush in a flash with my Romy. He lay on his side, sweaty and unconscious. "Romy! Wake up! Wake up!"

My father crawled in next to me, touching Romy with reservation. "Marlena, he's soaking wet—extremely sick. Oh, man, he may have done this on purpose."

"What do you mean?" I asked in a panic. All three men were half in the bush with me, and none of them said anything, but they all seemed to know something I didn't. "Please! What do you *mean*?"

Seeing as neither Trevor nor my father had the courage to break my heart, Jimmy softly said, "It means... he came here to die, Mar-cakes. Animals wander off when they know their time has come."

My eyes slammed shut as I begun to moan, completely overtaken with throbbing sensations attacking my organs. The thought of losing Romy was going to kill me, right there in front of my father, but then a memory passed though me. Mother Wolf.

He can't tell you yet... but he loves you, too.

Yet? My younger voice echoed in my head.

These men didn't know what I knew. Romy was possibly about to shift into something other than the wolf they were looking at. So I began the pointless but determined effort of trying to collect Romy into my arms and drag him from the shrubbery.

"What are you doing, little girl?"

"Taking my wolf home."

My father, Trevor, and Jimmy carried Romy all the way home.

CHAPTER FIVE

BEAUTY AND TORTURE BECOMING ONE

HAVING ROMY IN OUR BED in my arms was what kept me from falling apart. I couldn't sleep. I needed to stay awake to make sure he kept breathing. No TV echoed from downstairs. My parents slept. In the dark, I watched his fur rise and fall. I wondered what the hell was going to happen. *Will he turn human like his mom? Will I still be able to keep his secret?*

Mother Wolf's words came back to me. *He will never hurt you. He loves you too.* I remembered her telling me how *Sebastian*—I gasped when I remembered his real name—would need the moon's energy/gravity and space to change. My rickety bed was not going to do. Romy instinctively knew what his body needed, and I had just dragged him back home.

I thought about the cave having a wide-open entrance, where the moon could reach him, and he would still have cover. *I have to take Romy to the cave.*

When the moonlight crept through my window, his panting raced faster and faster. My heart pounded. His whimpers? They threw me right over the edge because now I knew his change was coming tonight and fast. I jumped out of bed, and I tried to wake him with no success. "Romy, please wake up. I think we have to go."

Nothing.

He felt hot and sweaty to the touch; his gray fur was matted. I whispered the only other word I could think of to wake him. "Sebastian."

Gray eyes slowly opened.

Gratitude poured from my heart, seeing my most favorite eyes, until I realized Romy didn't feel like a wolf to me. Something changed under his fur, telling me I was running out of time. "Romy? I think something's happening to you, and I think you need the woods for it to take place. Do you think you can walk?"

He blinked his eyes twice.

I ran to my desk to write a note to my parents.

Mom and Dad,

Please don't worry. I think Dad was right. Romy woke up and needs the woods. Please don't worry. Be home tomorrow.

Love ya,

Marlena

I rushed around my room, not knowing what to do next.

"Supplies?" I asked myself.

"Yes, good thinking," I answered myself.

I threw on a sweatshirt and grabbed an extra jacket and my backpack. Then I ran downstairs as quietly as I could for a flashlight, matches, water bottles, and snacks. I wasn't sure what a wolf-turned-*something* might be hungry for, but my Romy loved Pop Tarts for a midnight snack, so I grabbed the whole box and a banana. I don't know. Maybe I thought he was going to turn into a monkey.

Back upstairs in my room, I said to Romy, "I need you to follow me and trust me. I'm taking you to the cave." When he lifted his head, some sort of ghost's impression drifted directly over him, and he almost seemed… *human.* This almost-human shadow had an alarmed expression crossing its face that I'd never seen before. I blinked my eyes and saw Romy again. That was when I knew. Romy was turning into a man.

Anticipation, excitement and nervousness rushed through me as I tried to imagine Romy with legs, arms, and a mouth! *A way to talk to me!* Yes, Romy and I had found ways to communicate, but I sensed this would be so much more.

Haunted by the terror on the young man's face, I said, "No, I won't leave you there. I'll stay with you." I tried to assure him, in case Romy could hear me in that shadowed form.

He did, and he believed me. His slow and weak crawl out of bed told me so. I knew that at his pace, we weren't going to make it out of my room before he manifested into the young man I had just witnessed. So with my backpack strapped on, I put my arms around his ribs and helped my friend down the stairs. Quietly, we snuck out the back door. With a wolf living in their house and no fear of intruders, my parents usually slept like the dead, but with that wolf sick, I was afraid they would wake easily.

Once outside and fully immersed in the moonlight, something triggered in Romy, and he took off running across my yard. I hoped he was headed to the cave. Since my nighttime expert eyes had abandoned and left me behind, I pulled out my flashlight and chased the most important being in my life.

The cave was a forty-five-minute walk from my house, so I ran on and off for about twenty-five minutes before I heard torturous moaning. One should be scared of such a sound, but I knew who it was and followed the sounds tearing my heart apart. "Romy," I called out to him. "I'm here, Romy, looking for you."

I knew he had not made it to the cave. And when the moans tuned into pitiful howls, I ran with all I had, my heavy backpack bouncing on my back.

His shadow against the ground was what I saw first. His transformation was what I saw next. I jolted to a stop as I witnessed beauty and torture become one.

I could only see Romy's profile, not daring to interfere with what he had to do on his own. He went from all four paws to standing on his hind legs over and over while half howling and crying. His form kept shifting, but not in the gruesome ways I'd seen in movies. It was almost mystical, shadows of deception playing with my mind. His agonized cries told me nothing was happening to my mind, only his body and possibly his soul. Then male human screams erupted from the wolf howls as the form of the wolf violently danced with the form of a young man.

With every torturous moment and holler, fear ripped through me as his transformation ripped through him. Never had I seen someone suffer so, never witnessed such unimaginable pain. I loved Romy, which meant I already loved this young man who was fighting his way into the world. His misery was mine, and it made me hit my knees and slam my hands over my ears, wanting it all to end.

"Tell him not to fight it," Mother Wolf's words whispered from the distant memory.

My hands braced me from collapsing to the ground completely.

"Don't fight it! Let it happen, Romy!" My backpack slid, following my sudden movements.

The torment continued.

"Sebastian!" I screamed. "Embrace your calling!"

And that was it. Those words reached him, or maybe it was some deep-rooted instinct that should have been taught to him as he prepared for his transitional stage. Romy's arms flew out as his body surged through the final stage so dramatically that it arched backward, taking his full form to the balls of his paws/feet. All the shadows merged into place, and the naked body of a young man dropped to the ground.

Not taking the time to get up, I scrambled on my hands and knees to reach his side, terrified he might never wake, and I would be without him because I'd failed to tell him the message in time. "Romy! Romy! I'm here! I'm here!"

Once close enough, I stopped, realizing he might need to rest. Taking off my backpack, I watched his labored breathing. While he slept, steam rose from his naked form. I decided to inspect for anything that a wolf/human could have go terribly wrong, but what I saw was a body lying on its side, curled up, dripping in sweat. I watched his perfectly formed bare shoulders move with every tired inhale and exhale.

Long arms that were far from formed incorrectly had strong hands attached, lying out in front of him, an inch from my knees. Thick thighs were pulled to a stomach that, from what I could see, appeared to be etched in stone. Romy now had knees that could catch him every time he fell, calves that I was sure would prove to be worthy of any race, and feet that were prepared to carry him any distance.

Dark, damp hair partially covered the face I needed to see. All these years of him hidden inside Romy had me anxious about what was to be revealed. I leaned forward over his arms and dared myself to reach my shaky hand out and touch my friend. Softly, I pushed hair to the side.

I gasped.

He was simply the most stunning creature I had ever seen.

I don't know if I found him so beautiful because he simply was or because I loved him with every strand of emotion in my heart, but the kindness radiating from him that night instantly warmed my soul.

Full lips with a slender nose were perfectly in portion with cheekbones that invited me to see eyes that had yet to open. I knew if they were anything like his wolf eyes, they would be glorious, and if his soul was as sweet as my Romy's, I was about to meet one of the greatest in the world.

When he began to shiver, for the first time I remembered what season we were in and got a chill myself. I rushed through my backpack and pulled out my jacket, draping it gently over his nakedness. His eyelids fluttered. In barely a whisper, I said, "Romy?"

Eyelids slowly rose to expose me to the eyes of an angel. They were Romy's grays, yet a little lighter, almost hiding the cloud-like speckles.

Slowly, recognition washed over his face, and I couldn't stop my joyful tears. I didn't realize I'd had a hidden fear that this young man might not know me. But from the way he studied my face, I knew he did. This was somehow still my Romy.

His mouth opened. His lips moved as if trying to talk. His jaw tightened when no sound emerged. I softly touched his tense face and quietly cried. "It's okay. It's okay, Romy." I smiled through my tears and whispered, "Sebastian."

His eyes closed as his hands tried to move, his fingers reaching out. I looked at those long fingers and almost whimpered. "Do you want me to hold your hand?" His shoulders shook as his emotions took over, and I rushed to comfort him. I quickly took hold of his fingers and held his hand. My head lowered to his as I nuzzled to him as if he were still a wolf. "Embrace your calling, my dear friend."

His hand tightened on mine. He heard me.

We stayed like that for some time. He even slept some more. I let him until he began to tremble from the cold again. Touching his face as if he were my most precious gift, I whispered, "Romy, I need you to wake up now."

His eyes drowsily opened. I had to take a breath to accept his beauty before I spoke again. "I need to get you to the cave. Okay?"

A slight movement of his head was all I got. I took it for a yes.

Putting my backpack on, I told him, "I'm going to help you up, okay?" Another slight nod.

Lifting a man who weighs almost two hundred pounds and who has never had *feet* before was no easy task. In the first attempt, my jacket slid off, leaving him bare and exposed. He did not seem shy, and I was too worried to care, so I shoved the jacket back into my backpack before trying again. With my arm under his, I groaned and struggled as Romy forced his body to work. His new legs kept giving out from under him, slamming us back to the ground. I kept telling him it was okay and assured him I was fine every time his eyes begged me for forgiveness.

On my knees, I smiled at him while trying to brush dirt from his face. "Stop worrying about me. You're the one who has had a life-altering night—"

But I stopped speaking when his eyes closed. His face turned into my palm, inhaling deeply, as if he missed my comfort.

I'd kissed, petted, hugged, held, stroked, touched, and loved him for the past eleven years. I leaned to him as my other arm wrapped around his waist. "I'm here, Romy. I love you."

His arms came around my waist, just underneath my backpack, and his face nuzzled from one side of my face, under my chin, to the other side of my face. Maybe it looked odd, but it felt wonderful. It felt like my Romy, and I nuzzled him in return with an eagerness I could barely contain. Our lips brushed each other's with every passing, but it wasn't sexual. It was an affectionate moment that was incredibly intimate.

Rain began to fall, increasing the effects of the dropping temperature. I placed one hand to his cheek to get his attention because Romy never minded the rain. Eyes looked deep into mine, waiting for my next words.

"It's getting colder, and I don't know what your body needs yet, so I really want us in that cave."

Again, his eyes closed as his face turned to my palm, inhaling my scent, but this time, he nodded and looked back at me. I inhaled, preparing myself.

"Okay, here we go." I pushed my shoulder under his for as much support as I could offer. Success. We were finally standing, and I was now looking up to a young man somewhere over six feet tall with water dripping from his face. He shook and panted from the cold and muscle overload. Possibly it was from too much too soon, or whatever else goes along with changing your form *completely*.

We stumbled, and he groaned, but we didn't fall in the forming mud as Romy and I made our way to the cave through the rain. I was sure the cave would offer comfort, shelter, and the salvation my friend desperately needed. That was until we approached, and I acknowledged the fact that another animal might have made a home of our former napping area. In wolf form, Romy kept me safe. In this exhausted form, he needed me to be the protector for once. I shone my flashlight while trying to balance Romy on the shoulder I could offer.

After some inspection, I saw the cave was empty, and memories flooded my mind. *His puppy face as he grew...* Looking at his face now was astonishing.

I guided my friend inside the cave that had once seemed so big. Now it seemed cozy with the moonlight peeking through the clouds, my flashlight leading the way, and raindrops hitting the entrance with pitter-pat noises.

Once inside, the freezing Romy fell to his knees. I jolted down to the ground with him. I quickly took off my backpack and embraced him, trying to bring him some warmth. His arms came around my waist, and he shook. Into his neck and shoulder, I spoke. "Romy, I need to go collect wood and start a fire."

His arms tightened, telling me no. I figured it was because he was worried I would not come back until I realized what he might be trying to tell me. "It's raining?"

Slight nod.

"No fire with wet wood, huh?" When I chuckled, I realized I was also trembling, and that was probably another reason he wouldn't release me. Romy, always the protector.

My clothes were soaked through, and my Romy no longer had fur to warm himself or me. I thought about how many times I'd dressed in front of him and figured I had nothing he hadn't already seen. I began to let Romy go, but he was not willing to loosen his hold. I rubbed his face with mine, which started another round of intimate affections, but I got Romy to let me go so I could begin to remove my clothing.

As I lifted my undershirt over my head, Romy couldn't hold himself up without my support any longer and allowed a somewhat controlled fall to take place. When his eyes closed, my heart hammered in panic. "Romy!"

Without opening his eyes, he tried to reach for me. I rushed to finish taking off my pants. "I'm here, Romy. I'm coming to you."

When I was done, I quickly retrieved my jacket, ignoring the other items because I was so worried about him, and raced to lie by him to help ease his violent shaking. With my jacket covering over us, it felt surreal to press my naked body up against Romy's. Again, it didn't feel sexual. It didn't feel wrong because it wasn't. It was simply something I had never done before. Romy had no reservations, wrapping his arms firmly around me and intertwining his legs with mine. His face pillowed mine as he pulled me closer. Moments raced by as our hearts raced blood through our frozen bodies.

Once our shaking subsided a little, Romy pulled his face from under mine and touched his lips with his fingers, then his tongue, trying to tell me something.

"Thirsty?"

His nose rubbed mine, as if he was pleased that I understood him.

"I have water. Hold on." I reached over my head for my backpack and quickly pulled out a water bottle. Unable to open the bottle with one hand—and seeing how Romy was not releasing me anytime soon—I lifted my other arm over my head.

Unfortunately, this placed my breast directly in Romy's face. He was still nuzzling me with his eyes closed. Under my jacket, my wolf was now innocently rubbing his cold nose all over my chest. As I tried to ignore the *interesting* tickle my breast was experiencing, I continued to open his water, playfully telling him, "Oh Romy, you just took us to a whole other level without even knowing it." I brought the bottle to his lips. "Remember, this is different than licking out of a bowl."

I guess old habits are hard to break because when I brought the bottle to his mouth, his tongue came out immediately to retrieve some fluids. If he wasn't so parched and if it wasn't the prettiest tongue I'd ever seen, I would have teased him some more. Instead, I did my best to help him get as much water as possible into his mouth.

Two bottles later, my wolf's thirst was finally sated, and his exhausted body was demanding and forcing sleep. I made my backpack our pillow to share. With the moon bright and my flashlight on next to us, I was able to watch him sleep in my arms and allow all that had taken place that evening to sink in. Wet leaves gently blew into the cave as I wondered about what could have happened had he not embraced his calling. But he did, and he seemed just as happy as I that he had survived.

For tonight, it was just my wolf and me.

CHAPTER SIX

FASCINATION AND SIMPLICITY

A FAMILIAR NUZZLE, BUT WITH BARE skin instead of fur, woke me, and everything from the night before crashed through my mind. I jerked and opened my eyes in a hurry. "Romy?"

The sun had returned, the cave was bright, and he was... smiling.

My body relaxed at such a beautiful sight. In the light, I saw just how dark his hair really was and how his skin was gently kissed by the sun. Romy had made it through the change, and he had made it through his first night as a man. I inhaled a deep, thankful breath. "You're here, Romy... with me."

He happily snuggled close to me again. Then he pulled back slightly, and his mouth began to move. At first, I thought he might be thirsty again.

"M-Marley."

Romy said my name.

My eyes teared up with mixed emotions. My wolf had experienced a miracle that no one would ever believe and was strong and brave enough to try to speak again. And he chose *me* as his very first word. My heart was torn because that word meant so much and because it was his mother's last. She had passed before completing my name.

I caressed a face that could take two shapes and forms. I didn't know how or when, if ever again, he would be a wolf. "You remember your mother's last word?"

His eyes saddened at the mention of her passing, but he nodded yes.

"It was so long ago," I told him, "that I think a part of me forgot till this past year. Do you know what you are, Romy?"

His mouth struggled, but he spoke. "Y-y-your... f-friend."

Sudden joy busted through a barrier of worry, and I exploded with uncontrollable tears. "Yes, yes, you are my friend, Romy, and I am yours."

"F-for-e-ever."

I kissed him all over his face. "Yes, forever."

"M-Marley, w-will I ch-change b-back?"

"To a wolf?" I asked, sniffling.

He nodded.

"Your mother, Romy, she said… you have the ability, if you choose."

"H-how?"

The wolf asking the human how to be a wolf made me chuckle until my father's words echoed in my mind once again. I smiled and wiped some of my tears away. "Just *be* one."

His eyebrows came together in deep thought, and a shadow of a wolf began to appear, and the ghostly form imprinted onto Romy. I don't know why, other than being afraid of losing him, but I pleaded for him to stop the change.

"Romy, wait."

But his eyes were already closed, and he seemed not to be able to control it.

"Sebastian!"

His shadows disappeared, and his human form remained. Romy's eyes opened. Or were they Sebastian's eyes? I realized Romy was my wolf, and Sebastian was the human.

I nervously nodded because I wanted him to know I understood he heard me. "I was not ready for you to go… Sebastian."

"F-forever, M-Marley."

I wholeheartedly whispered my truth. "I love you."

"I love… you, t-too." His hand caressed my cheek.

In theory, it was a simple, tender moment, but Sebastian got a glimpse of his *hand* for the very first time. He stretched his fingers out and slowly flipped his palm to examine every little detail. I watched him in amazement.

Then I watched him as his hand gently came to touch my face again. He started to explore my skin. He touched the wetness under my eyes. He examined his thumb, rubbing my tear between his fingers. "I a-always wanted to do that." He looked at me. "Do y-you hurt?"

"No, I'm having happy tears."

He smiled again, and his expression showed his serious thought.

"What is it, Sebastian?"

"Do I h-have to s-stay here n-now?"

Not having my best friend with me would end me. "No, we stay together. We will just have to figure out how. I was told to keep you a secret. Maybe you should stay in wolf form in front of my parents, 'til we know what to do next."

He smiled, still in my arms with his head resting on my backpack. "I like th-them. S-So nice to me."

"They love you." I slowly ran my fingers through black, silky hair. "Your father's fur was black." Sebastian nodded. "Did he ever become human in front of you?"

"N-No. Neither d-did my mother till sh-she passed."

"Do you know why?"

"No... b-but both a-always watching."

"Think they were... nervous about something coming?"

Sebastian nodded.

"See? I hate to lie to my parents, but your mother must have had good reasons. If anyone finds out, what happen to her could happen to y—" I couldn't even finish that godawful sentence. "Do you miss them?" I hoped it wasn't a stupid, cruel question.

"S-Some, but not as much as before. I h-had you."

His stomach growling broke the serious moment, and I sat up in a hurry. Putting on my undershirt that had dried, I apologized. "Oh, Sebastian! You're hungry."

"M-must hunt."

"Umm, how about a Pop Tart?"

He slowly sat up.

"Do you hurt?"

"No... never... sat up... before."

"You're talking so much better already." I held up my sweatshirt to his chest. "This is never going to fit you. I didn't think to bring you clothes." I looked down and saw Sebastian in all his glory. I laid my sweatshirt over his lap. "Let's just let you be a little modest."

"Am I... ugly there?" he innocently asked.

"No, but seeing how I've never seen a—uh—*penis* in the flesh before, we shall keep it... under wraps, 'kay?"

"I have seen *you* unwrapped."

Cue blushing. "Uh, yeah, *that's* coming to an end."

"Why?"

I was lost for words. "Well, uh, it's not proper?"

"Why?"

"How about them Pop Tarts, huh?" I dug into my backpack before there could be any more questions about each other's genitalia. I handed him a package, and his long, inexperienced fingers fumbled with the wrapping. I showed him an example by ripping mine. "See?"

"Yes." He successfully opened his package. "F-feel like a child… leer-learning new things."

"Something tells me you will catch on quickly."

As he chewed, his expression showed him puzzled with new teeth.

"My parents are going to freak that we're gone, so we have to get back, but do you want to be… human again tonight? So we can talk more?" I was already missing this new side of Romy, and Sebastian had not even left me yet.

"I want to talk more… with you."

My heart did a pitter-patter. "Good."

"But b…fore we… go home, can we v-visit my mother?"

My hand grabbed my chest. "Yes, of course we can."

I wanted to get up and put my pants on, but the sun was bright. I was calmer and a little shy this time. "Sebastian, can you"—I pointed to a cave wall—"look over there while I finish dressing?"

"No," he answered simply while he kept chewing, inspecting his Pop Tart.

I was about to have my first argument with him. "Sebastian, it is needed."

"Don't agree. Can I finish your… Pop Tart?"

"And no more butt sniffing." That bothersome activity was going to be even more awkward picturing Sebastian's human nose between my cheeks.

He grinned at me.

I heard his unspoken answer loud and clear so I mumbled, "You're as stubborn as your wolf self." I handed him my leftover Pop Tart. "Here." I got up to dress in front of Sebastian as I always had with Romy. Sebastian did not seem fazed in the slightest by my tone, probably because Romy had heard it *plenty*.

I was putting my flashlight in my backpack when Sebastian decided to stand by himself. My sweatshirt fell off him, and I got to watch a naked Sebastian teeter and totter until he found sturdy feet. Unlike when I got dressed and Sebastian minded his Pop Tart, I did not. *My* eyes were traitors as they kept glancing at *all* that was teetering and tottering. I hadn't had years to become accustomed to the opposite sex's nudity the way Romy had. Not that he cared or even knew what he had been seeing this whole time, but I did. And my curiosity found Sebastian's body *fascinating*.

Sebastian stood proudly. "Look... I did it."

The saying, "Rome wasn't built in a day," was now making so much more sense to me. I glanced up at the smiling, naked wolf/human and found myself smiling grandly. "Yes, you did."

Neither of us spoke as we walked to his mother's gravesite. Sebastian seemed deep in thought, and I respected that. I wasn't sure I could even find the gravesite, and then I realized I didn't need to. Sebastian led me straight to an area where the grass was matted, as if someone had lain there *often*. I could barely swallow with the emotions choking me. "You-you still come here?"

He sat down. "Every day."

I sat next to him with shame in my heart. "I'm so sorry I forgot, Sebastian."

He ran his hand over the earth that covered his mother. "I understood. You did not mean to."

I whispered, "No, no I didn't."

The silence that followed wasn't uncomfortable. In fact, it was needed. We had experienced quite a night. I was surprised when Sebastian asked, "Do you think I made... my parents proud?"

That was such a heartfelt question. "Yes, very proud."

"I hope so," Sebastian quietly replied, looking at the ground.

"I know so, Sebastian. I saw how your mother's eyes adored you and how your father's spoke of pride every time he looked at his son."

Sebastian glanced at me. "Thank you."

"For what?" I gently asked.

"For c-coming with me. I like you... here."

I had never seen anyone so amazed at the *walking* process most of us humans took for granted, but as Sebastian conquered this simple act on the way back home, I realized how much I didn't appreciate the simple things. Sebastian was like a child, finding magnificent magic in what I had considered to be everyday normality.

"Everything looks so different from up here." Sebastian clearly had no concern about being completely nude. "It is...odd to have my nose not... lead me. Feel... half blind yet with different eyeballs."

Trying to keep my eyes at chest level and above, I reached for his hand. I just wanted to touch someone who found mystery and fascination in simplicity. He looked at our joined fingers. "Your hands are soft... yet you are strong."

I was too overcome to reply.

With his other hand, he reached out and touched a tree trunk. His fingers grazed the bark. "Not soft but...strong and sturdy. Like you."

I wondered what he had seen me do over the years to believe such words when describing me.

He inhaled deeply through his nose. "I don't get to smell... the details with this nose. I wish you could experience the dance."

I was a little confused. "The dance?"

"Yes, the way the dirt... flirts with the scents of the flowers. How nectar... teases and entices the tiny creatures of this grand forest and how the freshness of the trees... of the forest complement... the world."

I listened to his words, his understanding, in complete awe and with complete awareness of my unfortunate shortcomings.

As we came closer to where Romy became Sebastian for the first time, he calmly said, "They're looking for you."

Our walking and talking came to a stop. "Who? I don't hear anything."

"Everett, Trevor, and Jimmy."

"But I thought your senses were human now." I was perplexed.

"Can you smell them?"

"Uh, what? Smell—no."

"I'm suspecting even though I'm not in wolf form, my senses still surpass yours."

"Surpass? Wow, you really paid attention to schoolwork. How far are they from us?"

"Under a quarter of a mile, but they're moving fast."

I chuckled. "Quarter of a mile—I'm a great teacher."

Then I went quiet because it was time for Sebastian to become a wolf again. I felt anxious.

"Marley, once transformed, I will go and hunt."

Loving my new nickname, I nodded and tried not to become emotional. "Pop Tarts didn't do the trick, huh?" He looked at me with sympathy, so I asked, "What is it?"

"I feel your sadness but wonder why you feel so."

"What if—what if you don't turn back to... this?"

"Then you shall love me as Romy only, and Sebastian will fade away."

Tears brimmed.

He touched my face. "But I don't feel that is what will happen. Forever, Marley."

He backed away. The ghost took hold, and within a couple of seconds, Sebastian was once again my Romy. My chest felt torn because seeing Romy again reminded me of how much I loved him, too. With immense gratitude, I watched him circle me, his fur brushing my hips, before he ran away to feed.

As I broke the tree barrier of the clearing, my father, Trevor, and Jimmy entered on the other side, clearly following my tracks with Hound in the lead. When they saw me, they ran to my side. But one look at my tears and they jolted to a stop. They looked around but saw no wolf. My father grabbed his chest. "Romy?"

I smiled through more happy tears. "No, he's okay. Romy will be just fine."

Three grateful men sighed in relief.

After I stretched the truth, saying Romy had had a rough night but was now back to himself, Trevor and my father got to talking and were exiting the clearing. I looked back to see Hound examining the ground—something I did *not* want. "Gonna be a gentleman and walk me home?" I called out.

Jimmy looked at me, eyebrows crunched together. He finally pulled himself away and jogged to catch up with me. He whispered, "You okay?"

"Much better now that Romy is well," I answered, hoping he would drop the subject.

"Who's the heavy man you struggled with last night?"

Lying didn't come naturally to me. I looked at the ground. "Uh, I don't know what you're talking about."

Jimmy watched me for a moment as we walked and sarcastically said, "Yeah, I'm seeing that."

Chapter Seven

God, Feelings, and Happy Tears

I WAS GIDDY, EXCITED, RELIEVED, AND most of all, happy in a deep part of me that I was not aware existed, not till it started to burn with a desire for *life*. How many people can say that? Not many. How many people are excited to come home after a long day at work or school because they're living a life they adore? See, that was just it! Maybe what my life had become was not for everyone. Having a wolf/human live in our home was, well, challenging at times, but that challenge was what began more growth for me. I fell in love with the gray eyes of my furry best friend, and when challenges arose, I fought hard for what I believed in: my wolf and me.

My parents could not stop grinning as I ate my dinner, as though I were six again and had just been promised a chocolate factory of my very own. I laughed at them staring at me. "*What?*"

"Our daughter is glowing," Mom said with a delighted smile.

My father shook his head. "Who would have ever known a pet could mean so much to someone?"

Just then, a howl sounded at our back door, announcing an evening entry. "He's home!" I *ran* to answer that call and opened the door to be tackled to the ground and licked with a frenzy that had my parents on their feet, hugging the wolf that had changed our lives for the better.

Standing in my room with my ear at my door was all I could do. I was desperate for my parents to finally go to sleep. When the house was quiet for a while, I turned to face my wolf but what I found was a young man smiling at me. He was sitting on the floor, patiently waiting. My heart slammed against my rib cage as I sighed. "Sebastian."

I was relieved. He was able to be Sebastian again.

"Marley. Happy to see me?"

No words were needed to explain how happy I was. It was all over my smile.

I gasped. "You're in pants!"

He looked guilty. "I stole them off a clothes line, transformed, threw them through your window, then transformed and howled at the back door. Are you angry at me?"

I sat in front of him. "No, but I would prefer we find another way in the future to get you some clothes. Oh, I know! My mom said she put together a bag of clothing to be dropped off for donation. I'll look through it for some of my dad's old clothes. We'll hide them in my closet. You know I do my own laundry, so my mom will never notice yours in with mine."

We sat and whispered for hours. Sebastian had many questions—as did I. I learned he was extremely intelligent with an incredible capacity to learn. He knew algebra and the math course I was presently in, along with all of my other subjects, and he was *hungry* for more.

Romy and I had a connection and understanding of our affections for each other, but Sebastian and I had to now learn about other beliefs and subjects. He had many questions about God.

"So he lives in the sky?"

I pondered on how to answer this important question. "I don't know. Some say so. Some believe he lives in *everything*."

"Even me?"

I smiled. "If God truly does exist, yes, Sebastian, I believe you would be proof of God being a part of everything." His head tilted, waiting for more explanation. I quietly giggled, recognizing that simple head tilt as such a Romy gesture. "You... a gift to me. Your friendship as Romy has fulfilled my life in measures I will not pretend to be able to judge. And now? I think that's the beauty of it. Who knows?"

"Who knows what?"

"Where we are headed." I looked at my door, realizing I was getting excited and too loud. I whispered, "There's a world to experience, and now? Now you and I can experience it together."

He nodded. "I am limited on what I have seen but would love to see more. Could I get a job? Or go to school?" He leaned forward. "Oh, college?"

I put my finger over my mouth to remind him to be quiet. "Well, yes and no. You need a social security number for some of those things."

"What is that?"

I tried to muffle a laugh. "My father says it's a way for the government to keep track of business that's not theirs, but it's a number that is given to you, usually at birth so that, well, I guess so that the government can keep track."

"Can you get one when you are older?"

"I believe so, but you still need some kind of proof of where you came from. Or maybe there's a way around that."

"I will search the internet while you're at school."

A visual of Romy typing away at my keyboard had me giggling again. Sebastian pulled me to him. "I have always loved your laughter—so many different versions of it."

When I realized I was in his arms, I found myself pulling away. His hands followed my retreat. "Why do you change when I'm Sebastian?"

I knew it would take some time to become accustomed to Sebastian's upfront questions and statements. I looked down, feeling a little shameful. "Uh, not too sure."

"When I'm a wolf, you hold me endlessly—and last night. But this morning and now, you hold back. Have I done something to upset you?"

"*What?* No," I said, a little embarrassed and confused that his bare, beautiful chest was capturing my attention. My unexpected reactions caused me conflict because I was seeing him so differently. That had me wondering how Sebastian was viewing me. *Will he now be like other boys?* I tried to explain something I didn't understand myself. "It's because when you're Romy, you're my... Romy?"

I was hoping that would clear things up for us both.

"Am I not your Romy now?"

Not shockingly, it didn't.

My eyes closed, and my hand rested over my chest. He sounded hurt. Sebastian's raw, unaltered view of *us* was liberating and scary at the same time. When I could not answer, I realized that *I* was the one making this ugly, not beautiful.

"I apologize if I've hurt your feelings. It's just, I'm not sure what *I'm* feeling. Maybe I have to remind myself you are not like other boys—wanting things from me I'm not ready to give." It was a crappy reply, but I truly wasn't sure what was happening inside me.

"What do they want from you, Marley?"

That answer told me he was nothing like the guys at school and that I had just walked myself into a minefield. "Uh, that's a discussion for another time."

He nodded in thought. "Hurt my *feelings*?"

I was not embarrassed about this question. "Yes, feelings." I touched his chest to show him where. "What you feel here."

I was a little taken aback with how nice it felt to touch him like that. My body and mind struggled to communicate when I touched his stomach next. "And here."

My fingers refused to leave his skin, so I stared at them and their misbehavior as my heart thumped faster than usual. I took a sharp intake when his hand grabbed mine, holding it to his stomach. He smiled. "Oh, you mean love."

My jaw dropped. With my fingers still enjoying his warmth, I asked, a little breathlessly, "Is that what you feel... here?"

"I think so. I learned what love was when every time you hugged me and told me you loved me, I felt something here and here." He pulled my hand to his chest, forcing my fingers to unfold, lie flat, and touch more of him. And then, as if a fire had been ignited in his soul, he said, "Something so wonderful that it fed my whole body with a food I could not find in the woods. Only you make me feel this way. Love. Are those happy tears, Marley?"

I could barely speak with how much his words and touch affected me. Never had anyone ever spoken to me with such conviction. "Yes, happy tears because I thought I had so much to teach you, but now I see... it's *you* who will be teaching me."

After that tender moment, I never again held back my affection from Sebastian. Neither my heart nor body would allow it. That night, we grew, and I learned that love is a simple, wondrous feeling to feed your body and soul. If what someone is giving you feels bad, it is not love.

Sebastian asked if he could stay in his human form for a little longer so he could hold me. He said, as a wolf, he couldn't squeeze me in return while we slept, but he'd always wanted to. I said yes, as my heart warmed in a way I hoped everyone on earth could someday experience.

In bed, his arms circled me from behind and spoke volumes of his true feelings. I internally giggled. For once, he did not complain about me blanketing him.

In the dark, he spoke with his chin resting on my shoulder. "Your scent has always been my favorite. I can pick it up anywhere."

Maybe not the words girls dream of hearing when being held by a man, but they were still special to me.

"Marley, when you cry, I feel something *different* inside. Is that love, too?"

"I guess, in a way, it is. When the person you love hurts, you hurt, too. When we thought you were sick, I hurt for you. When you were experiencing pain and fear with the beginning of your transformation, I felt that pain and fear with you."

Sebastian thought for a moment. "Marley, do you feel this with Trevor?"

"Here's the thing. What you have taught me in such a short amount of time is that love *is* feelings, and there are different levels and degrees to these feelings—like there are different levels and degrees of love. So, yes, I feel these things with him, but with you, Sebastian, it is life or death."

"Life or death?"

"Yes. If you live, I live. If you die, I die."

CHAPTER EIGHT
BATTERED AND TATTERED SURPRISES

B Y MORNING, SEBASTIAN WAS ROMY, and a warm, wet snout breathed heavily in my ear. His long wolf legs hung over me.

Sebastian was one of the most fascinating people to walk this earth, but Romy could never be replaced. I easily fell back into our routine. Getting ready for school, I pulled clothes out of the closet and asked the furry beast on my bed what he thought. I always got two enthusiastic barks. He simply thought I looked great in everything. Who was I to argue with someone as brilliant as he?

Romy walked me to my bus stop. I told the wolf, "I'll miss you today." Two barks.

The bus pulled up. Trevor and Jimmy lowered their windows. Trevor yelled, "Romy! You're alive, ya son-of-a-bitch! Damn good to see you, D.O.G!"

One bark. Romy was a wolf.

I kissed Romy's head and then happily marched up the bus steps. Trevor spoke over Carrie, who was practically in his lap, trying to hold his attention. "Ya look much better, girl."

I sat with Jimmy, kissed his cheek, then looked behind me. "The world, T. Means the world what you two did for me." Trevor grinned mischievously, so I asked, "What?"

"You called me T."

I won't lie and say it didn't sting to see Trevor with Carrie, but he was making up for lost time, and where panties dropped, T was found. My panties were still intact, and that made me proud of myself. I hadn't surrendered something I happened to value because someone wanted it. No, not just someone—an old friend who meant so much to me. But in the end, his hormones outweighed what I needed. Trevor was ready to experiment sexually. I was not and was truly thankful he was honest and let me go.

As the week progressed, it was evident Carrie was not T's only conquest. At my locker, Jimmy put his arm around me, looking at all the criers gathering in the hallway. "I'm gonna start call'n' them the Battered and Tattered Ts."

I shouldn't have, but I burst out laughing, relieved to not be a Battered and Tattered T. "Let's eat. I'm starving!"

Jimmy kept his arm around me as we headed to the cafeteria. "Well, you're not in luck. It's pizza day, which means dog day."

"I don't know why you say the pizza tastes like a wet dog. Do you understand how that sounds?"

"What I *imagine* a wet dog to taste like. Big difference, smartass."

Romy's excitement when I got home from school was normal, of course, and his constant rubbing and claiming me were also routine. And apparently swatting his snout away was also going to continue. Sebastian, on the other hand, complaining about certain scents on me was something that took me by surprise. From time to time, I would forget that Sebastian and Romy were one and the same. The first time it happened, I stood still, a little perplexed, as Sebastian rubbed himself all over me in my bedroom. "What are you doing?"

"I don't know, but his scent on you is making me feel… odd. Can't describe it without sounding selfish."

"Huh, okay. Uh, how do you know it's a he?" I asked, still not moving and still being rubbed on.

"Because I know Jimmy's scent. It just never *irritated* me before."

And then it happened. Sebastian's nose headed south. I caught his chin, my fingers leading him north again until he was upright. "What the *hell* do you think you are doing?"

His eyes were glassed over, and a shadow of Romy flashed right in my palm. I gasped but couldn't move my hand from such magic. Then his expression faded, and Sebastian winced. "Not sure. Just feel a pull to make sure no unfamiliar scent is—"

"Stop right there." I released him.

"But I can't explain the need to know—"

I put up my other palm. "Not happening."

"Marley, please. You won't let me inspect while I'm Romy."

"Inspect? What am I? A rack of lamb?"

Sebastian looked down at his trembling hands. This was clearly an issue for Sebastian and causing havoc between his human and wolf form, so I compromised. I grabbed his hands to settle whatever was happening inside him. "Okay, how about I allow Romy—I can't believe I'm doing this—only *Romy* a quick sniff when I get home from now on."

Sebastian's eyes closed. "Deal."

"But it has to be a speedy event because this is humiliating."

"I will not linger, promise."

I rolled my eyes. "I don't even understand the importance to you."

His eyes glossed over again. "I don't know." He bent his knees.

I stepped away, causing Sebastian to hit the floor, growling at my denial. Walking away from him, I laughed over my shoulder. "Growl all you want. Still not happening."

So every day after school, Romy would rub on me downstairs as my mother stood in her apron with a disapproving look as a *speedy* sniff took place. Then in my room, Sebastian would rub while I waited. Once the new routine was complete, Romy or Sebastian was all mine.

Sometimes there were parts of Sebastian that I could do without. Entering my room, I loudly whispered, "Sebastian! Did you do another stinky?"

"Sorry."

I shut my bedroom door behind me and handed him a bowl of chili. Sebastian's eyes lit up. "Marley! Thank you." He eagerly took the bowl. "But you do understand passing gas is a natural necessity, right?"

"Can we not discuss this while you're eating my mother's famous chili?"

He shrugged, his mouth full of chili. "And I don't believe they smell bad."

"I'm taking the bowl back." I reached for it. Sebastian chuckled and, avoiding my attempts, shoved more chili down his throat.

Later, once we were settled for the night, I appreciated how much easier it was to share a bed with Sebastian. I didn't have to compete for space on the worn mattress. Thinking about competing for space had me thinking of Trevor and all his newfound conquests. "How come he changed so drastically?" I tried to talk softly so my sleeping parents wouldn't wake.

The moon shone through our bedroom window, delicately lighting the room.

Sebastian lay on his side, spooning me. "Don't think *he* did. It's his *actions* that have changed."

"Huh?" I stared at my ceiling.

"Maybe you're not understanding Trevor's true form."

"What true form?"

"His alpha one."

"Oh, you mean his asshole form," I teased as I rolled to face Sebastian.

Under his long bangs, Sebastian's face scrunched up. "Asshole—what an insult to a needed part of your body. Have humans really thought about that? What would happen if your *asshole* refused to do its job? I think being called an asshole should be a compliment. It makes you one who is willing to sacrifice for the good of the team. Quite heroic, in my opinion."

Silence.

"You just ruined a perfectly good cuss word for me, Sebastian."

He kissed my forehead. "Being alpha shouldn't mean being an asshole—using your definition, of course. Being an alpha means watching over your own, dying for them if needed to keep them safe. Keeping them in line, but with respect, not cruelty. At least, that's how my father was with my mother and me. A nip on the neck was meant as a reminder, not a promise of future pain."

"Umm, I see what you're saying, but what does this have to do with Trevor?"

"Remember that wolf program we watched on TV?"

"Uh, yeah, that was a while back, but go on."

"Well, that alpha reminded me of my father's ways, and over the years, I have witnessed Trevor constantly trying to be yours and Jimmy's alpha. Trevor may not be aware of it, but he's trying to keep you in line with his actions."

As days melted into weeks, Sebastian and I effortlessly submerged ourselves into our own little world. I couldn't prevent it. There were so many things to learn and explore with Sebastian, such as how much he loved doing homework with a pen in his hand. Sounds simple, but to watch his excitement enthralled me. Writing was challenging, but he pushed himself to teach his hand to do what his mind commanded. His stern facial expressions showed his level of concentration. As soon as a click in the communication between his body and mind would take place, Sebastian would have another ability conquered. Soon, it was hard for me to believe he had only recently learned how to write.

Time passing went unnoticed. I could only focus on Sebastian's positively limitless ambitions. I wondered if his hunger for knowledge—his constant request for more input—was what Helen Keller's teacher experienced as Helen finally began grasping the world she lived in. *Was she as entranced as her student? Like me?*

Sebastian's proud smile should've warned me when he told me he had a surprise. I excitedly tried to get information from him, but he was sly as a wolf—no pun intended—and told me I had to wait.

Every evening, another secretive late-night talk took place. Sebastian decided he believed in the thing called God because whenever he was in the forest, he sensed he was never alone. He told me that he was realizing he felt the same way in his human form. "There's something all around us, Marley. I think the people who say he lives everywhere are correct."

I inhaled deeply, thanking whatever brought this magnificent being into my life.

We only had one close call with my parents, and that was when Sebastian forgot to wake and become Romy in the middle of the night. I guess our late nights had finally caught up with us because neither of us woke when my dad came up the stairs one morning. I was late getting up for school, so my dad opened my door in two nanoseconds after one knock. The male body spooning me flew backward and tumbled to the floor.

My father's voice boomed, "What the hell?" But Romy's furry face peeked over the mattress to face the door.

I was sure one of my dad's old pants were ripped and on the floor. With no time to undress, Romy's wolf form had shredded Sebastian's clothing.

My dad grabbed his chest. "Oh, Romy! You scared the shit out of me. I thought a boy was in my daughter's bed." My father looked at me. "Gracing school with your presence today, little girl?" He walked away, saying, "Thought I was gonna have to spill some young man's blood—being in bed with my baby."

My mother's voice echoed from the kitchen. "Who was in her bed, Everett?"

Headed down the stairs, my father answered, "The only male allowed, thank God."

On rare occasions, Mom and Dad treated themselves to a night out. This allowed for more learning with Sebastian. I came down the stairs after a shower to encounter a panicked new human and a laundry room in shambles. Sebastian was desperately trying to put back the incredible amount of bubbles overflowing out of the washing machine. I rushed in. "Sebastian, what happened?"

"I thought I would help with your chores, but this machine is very angry with me!"

I turned off the angry machine and grabbed some towels as I explained to Sebastian that one scoop of laundry soap would suffice—not four.

He soaked up bubbles with a towel I handed him. "I feel it is only right to help you earn your allowance since you spend it on my clothes."

My mom would send me to town on an errand, and I would take advantage of sales for Sebastian. His thoughtfulness continued to amaze me. "That is so sweet, Sebastian, but maybe we should start you with a task such as dusting?"

The adventure of his dusting ended with his brute strength breaking one lamp and knocking over another.

"Sorry, Marley."

I just laughed, following him around with a broom.

We moved to dishes. Somehow, Sebastian found this to be an exhilarating experience. The fact that you could put dirty dishes into a machine and then pull clean ones out had him pointing. "I've always wanted to know, who is in there scrubbing?"

Oh, boy.

Another night, my parents left to enjoy alone time. Romy became Sebastian, and we opted to snuggle on the couch and watch a movie. Eating snacks like the mischievous teenagers we had become was way more fun than cleaning a waterlogged laundry room.

"What is this called, Marley?"

Crunch, crunch. "Caramel popcorn."

Crunch, crunch. "It's wonderful."

"Sebastian? Is there any food you *don't* like?"

He smiled with a full mouth. "Not yet."

The TV showed a kissing scene that was on the lighter side. Sebastian popped in more of our snack. "Did you like kissing Trevor?"

The question stunned me a little, but I recovered and understood Sebastian just wanted more data to learn from. I leaned my head back to rest on the couch. "Umm, yes, but it wasn't like I've seen on TV." He looked at me with a puzzled expression. "Well, watch that kiss." I pointed to the screen. The kiss was building in intensity. "Don't they look enraptured?"

Sebastian watched intently. "They feel something because of the kiss?"

"Yes, desire."

"You didn't feel desire?"

I took a deep breath with a touch of regret. "No, no desire, just a need."

"Need?"

I stared at the TV with sadness because I wanted to be swept away with emotions. "Yeah, a need to please Trevor. I guess my needs were never met, huh?"

When I got no answer, I looked at Sebastian, who had stopped chewing and stared at the TV, completely distracted. I followed his gaze and saw the kiss was now full on. Mouths were opening, and after the guy kissed his girlfriend with exposed tongue, Sebastian—who couldn't pull his eyes from what he was watching—asked, "Can I touch your tongue?"

"*What?*" I shrieked.

A deep chuckle rumbled in his chest. "Please? I want to know what it feels like."

"You're not sticking your tongue in my mouth, Sebastian."

He thought for a second while swallowing his popcorn. "Can I touch it with my finger?"

I made a face that had him laughing out loud.

"Come on! Marley, let me touch!" He leaned toward me with his finger sticking out, ready to prod my mouth. I slapped his hand away, laughing. He pleaded. "One touch and I'll leave you alone. *Please?*"

I rolled my eyes. "This is so weird." I opened my mouth.

He looked so inquisitive as he stuck his finger in my mouth. Gently, his finger rubbed the top of my tongue. His eyes widened. "Wow, it's so... smooth." He kept touching. "Oh Marley, let me lick you there."

I pulled away. "Do you have *any* idea how wrong that sounds?"

He just kept smiling in amazement. "Want to touch mine?"

"*And* it's getting worse."

He opened his mouth, sticking out his tongue, and tried to talk. "Ca on, tuch et. Yu know yu wunt ta."

I did want to touch him. "I've already touched a tongue."

He sat up straight. "With your finger?"

"Well, no—"

He opened his mouth again and leaned toward me. "Ca on, et's cuul!"

Curiosity won, and I timidly stuck my finger in Sebastian's mouth for an examination. He patiently waited as I touched and touched. I was just amazed feeling life under my touch. "You're right. Silky." I retracted my finger.

Sebastian proudly smiled. "Told ya so. Now tongue on tongue?"

"No."

"Why?" He whined like a child.

"'Cause I said so," I replied like a parent—even though I was quite sure kissing Sebastian wouldn't exactly be a miserable experience. He might not be Hollywood material, but I found him handsome nevertheless.

Suddenly, I remembered something. I jumped up from the couch. "I almost forgot!"

I ran up the stairs. Sebastian followed. He was becoming very quick on his feet. It was as if his wolf begged to be set free and run, so his human form had no choice but to become faster.

After digging in my backpack, I said, "Go back down to the couch, and close your eyes."

"Why, Marley?"

"And don't open them 'til I say."

Sebastian ran down the stairs and waited—well, ate more popcorn with his eyes closed. I removed the bowl from Sebastian's grasp then sat down. "Put your hands out."

He did, and I placed his surprise in his open palms. "Open my eyes now?"

"Oops. Sorry. Yes, open your eyes."

He did and smiled in realization. "Marley, my first pair of shoes."

A pair of sneakers, size twelve.

"I'm sorry I didn't think of it sooner."

Sebastian started sticking them on. "I can't wait to see what they feel like."

"No! You have to put these socks on first, or they will get stinky."

"You hate when I make stinkies."

His mature, deep voice sounded out of place while making a childish comment. I chuckled. "Boy, do I."

Just the thought of his catastrophic events had me plugging my nose with one hand and handing him socks with the other. Sebastian handled the socks as if they might do tricks at any moment, but eventually we got his feet into them, and his first pair of shoes was on.

"Let's go run, Marley!"

Yes, we, Sebastian and Marley, ran through the woods under the moon with his new pair of shoes. And that is how Romy, Sebastian, and I spent the days and nights: running through the woods, learning each other—growing into young adults. The leaves eventually turned to beautiful fall colors, and soon fell to the earth, leaving the trees bare. Romy's fur thickened, and his appetite grew. Snow on the ground was the only thing that slowed us down—well, *me* down.

My teeth chattered. "I don't want to go inside. It will be hours before we get to talk again."

Sebastian had already taken off his shirt to prepare for his transition. His arms circled me. "It is the better alternative. Otherwise, I will have to thaw out my Marley popsicle."

His embrace was so warm it entranced me. "Hmm?" His hot, bare skin next to my frozen cheek closed my eyes involuntarily.

"Well, you upper half seems happy now, but what about your toes experiencing frostbite?"

His scent sang to my nostrils as I snuggled to him. "Who needs toes?"

Sebastian's laugh echoed in the woods. He grasped my face in his heated palms, lifting my closed eyes to his. "I love you and don't like to hear your heartbeat change when you're this cold."

My eyes opened as my head still tilted. "You can hear my heart?"

"Always."

It felt like time stilled to allow me this extraordinary moment. Magnificent gray eyes looked so deeply into mine, causing my heart to—

"See? Picking up speed. I think your heart is stressed trying to keep your body warm."

"*Uh.*"

Sebastian's lips descended. He kissed the tip of my nose. "Feels like ice." Then he stood up straight. "You heart is thundering, Marley!"

"Uh—"

He grabbed my hand and began gently dragging me away. "Home we go."

I stumbled behind him, wondering why the thought of him kissing me had me so flabbergasted. Clueless Sebastian kept marching in the opposite direction from where I wanted to go. I wasn't getting a say in the matter, and that was annoying me. "Home we go," I complained as I lazily followed. "Always wanting me home if one little thing seems off to you."

He pushed a branch aside for me. "The only thing off is your blood circulation."

Not altogether true.

The long cold season made Sebastian and me appreciate spring once it arrived. The sun on our faces was just as bright as the light that shone from inside Sebastian. "So you have no school for a whole week?"

"Yep! Spring break is almost here. Can you entertain me?" I teased and pointed to the trunk we were scaling, deep in the woods. "Now focus!"

I began to show Sebastian—to the best of my abilities—how to climb a tree. It had been many years since such an attempt. "See, you reach up like this and grab a branch," I explained as my arm stretched over my head. "Then pull yourself up while having your feet try to defy gravity" I grunted during the next part while I struggled through my poor example. "And walk up the tree trunk—ah!" I screamed as I fell but stopped when I landed in safe, strong arms. Being cradled, I looked at Sebastian and shrugged. "Like so."

"Hmm. How about you stand on my shoulders to avoid more humiliation."

It was a childhood activity that I'd grown out of long ago and had thought was in the past until I sat in the tree—where I had been hoisted courtesy of Sebastian—and witnessed the pure joy of the young man slipping and sliding in his new—now old—shoes, until he managed to climb on a limb and appreciate yet another view of life.

"It feels like belonging, resting in the arms of a friend."

I smiled, knowing his only example was me, and observed as his long back leaned against the strong trunk, and his legs effortlessly lounged over the sturdy branch supporting his body. Yes, Sebastian was being cradled by a friend. Nature. And he was appreciating every moment. I appreciated every moment I got to watch Sebastian. He seemed to be at such ease simply being either Sebastian or Romy. Or so I thought.

While I was pulling a book out of my locker, getting ready for third period, Jimmy approached me. "So, the Spring Dance?"

I rolled my eyes. "Can you believe people actually go to that?"

"You know you're a girl, right?"

"Do you know that I've hung with two guys named T and Hound all my life and have been ruined when it comes to girly stuff?"

Jimmy laughed. "So now this is my fault?"

"You stand guilty as accused. I'm not going to a dance—ever!"

"Excuse me," someone said from behind me. "Could you tell me where room one-twenty-two is?"

I turned around and made an unrecognizable sound in my throat.

Jimmy stared at my odd reaction, while *I* stared at... *Sebastian*.

Chapter Nine
Correct and Questionable Conclusions

"Oh, Jesus," I whispered, as I stared into my favorite light grays smiling back at me. Immersed in a normal school day, I never saw this coming and felt adrenaline racing through me.

"Do you know this guy?" Jimmy asked with some agitation.

"Umm..." I was too astonished to give Jimmy much of my focus. I could only see Sebastian as my mind tried to comprehend how he was standing in my school.

Jimmy faced Sebastian, since he was not getting answers from me. "Who are you?"

"My name is Sebastian. I am new here." Sebastian studied me.

All I could muster up was "You're new? *Here?*"

Jimmy asked me, "How do you know someone *I don't know* that you know?"

Ignoring Jimmy and his confusing question, my wolf proudly answered me. "Yes. I'm a *student.*"

Jimmy kept watching Sebastian and me stare at each other. "Where do you know him from?"

"A student?" I grabbed my chest. "A-are you going to be okay?" I asked my wolf.

"Are you?" Jimmy asked me with sarcasm.

Sebastian kept smiling but finally broke our stare to look around the hallway full of students. "Everything is so *much.*"

Instantly, I was worried and tried to assure him. "It's okay. I will walk you to your class and, and, and *help* you."

Jimmy looked perplexed. "What? *Why?* The kid is smiling from ear to ear."

In a panic, I explained to Jimmy. "He's *new!*"

"Not to the world, Mar-cakes. What's going on here?"

This extremely reasonable question became a brick wall I ran into. The realization of what Sebastian had done slammed into me. He had opened himself up to the public and was now exposed to all these questions—ones I had no answers to. And since Jimmy was waiting for a reply, I couldn't ask Sebastian what the hell he was thinking.

After a deep, not-so-calming breath, I said, "I owe you an apology, Jimmy."

"Why do you need to apologize?"

"Because I lied to you. I *do* know Sebastian."

Jimmy rolled his eyes. "You don't know how to lie. The only time I think you ever did was—" He stopped in thought. Then, with reservation, he said, "Was the night Romy was sick."

I could not get air into my lungs as Jimmy put all the pieces together. This was it, the moment I'd dreaded for months, the moment I could no longer keep my Romy safe as I'd promised Mother Wolf.

Jimmy nodded in a surrender of the unbelievable truth. "He's the guy I saw in the tracks. He helped you with Romy?"

I blinked. *What?*

Believe it or not, I was somehow surprised that Jimmy didn't guess that Sebastian *was* Romy—some sort of werewolf. I had been living with this miracle for so long I thought others would easily jump to the correct conclusions.

As if it all made sense now, Jimmy told Sebastian, "You must be a hunter and came across Mar-cakes and her sick wolf and helped them." He offered his hand for a shake. "Thank you so much. She was so upset."

It wasn't the case, but I was relieved that Jimmy's conclusion made sense and that he was satisfied with it. And best of all, it wasn't a lie! Sebastian *did* help me with Romy—in a way, which *did* help me. And Sebastian *was* a hunter—in the form of Romy. It was close enough for me to inhale with relief, and agree with Jimmy. "Yes, that is *exactly* what happened."

Sebastian hesitantly shook Jimmy's hand. "You're welcome?"

Jimmy looked pleased with the situation and had only one question. "Why didn't you tell me that night?"

"Uhhh... umm..." I blew out an exasperated breath.

The bell rung as Jimmy smacked my shoulder. "Oh, my God! You like this kid!"

"Uhhh…"

Once again, Jimmy was filling in the blanks wonderfully on his own. "And you didn't want to say anything because of Trevor being there and all that had just gone down with you two—'cause that would've been awkward as hell."

A slight moment of shock ticked by.

I awkwardly shrugged. "You know me so well."

Jimmy excitedly threw his arms around my shoulders and started walking with me. "Now that we're late *anyways*, let's walk your new *boy toy* to class."

I stuttered, "B-boy toy?"

Jimmy told Sebastian, who was now walking with us, "One-twenty-two? Mrs. Harold's a bitch. Sorry 'bout your luck, dude. Hey, so if you're in her class, you're a senior? Another to add to our pack. Rock on, soldier."

Sebastian stated, "Oh, I'm not a soldier, and I don't understand how to rock on."

Jimmy mumbled in my ear, "When did Mrs. Harold start teaching Special Ed?"

I elbowed Jimmy in the ribs. "Sebastian, if you're a senior, you have the same lunch period as we do. Will you eat lunch with us?"

"Yes, I love food." Sebastian winked at me. I didn't even know he knew *how* to wink, and was shocked when I found it sexy as hell. "Where would I find the cafeteria?"

I felt as if I was sending my baby into a war zone. Let's face it, school cafeterias are. "It's actually next period, so I will take you. Can you meet me at my locker?"

"Yes."

"Here's your classroom." I pointed. "I can help you get settled—"

With his arm still around my shoulders, Jimmy said, "*And* we're out. See ya, Boy Toy." He practically dragged me away from my wolf, mumbling, "Let a man be a man, Mar-cakes."

Under my breath, I muttered, "Talk about your full-circle moments."

"What?"

"Nothing."

In my class, I couldn't focus on a word my teacher was saying. All I could do was think of Sebastian and wonder *how* and *why* he was now a student at my high school. I guess I knew and understood *why*, but not the how. Then it hit me: *his surprise*. For a moment, I was angry with him. He was taking such a chance by exposing himself, but then I felt sorry for him. This was probably a dream come true. Most kids want *out* of school; Sebastian desperately wanted *in*.

Watching the clock on the wall made it feel as if time had practically stopped altogether. "Come on!" I whispered loudly and impatiently to the minute hand that crept along. Everyone stared at me but I didn't care. When that bell rang, I was out the door in a blur.

I opened my locker, shoved my crap in, and took off to find my poor wolf. I was supposed to wait there, but I was sure Sebastian was most likely shaking with fear. Or at least that's what I'd envisioned happening. What *really* was taking place was a girl on each side of Sebastian, clinging to his strong arms that had only touched *me* up to this point. I had to admit I didn't like it. At all.

And the fact that these two girls were part of the Battered and Tattered club was not helping. I knew what they were willing to offer and could still feel the sting of T happily accepting. They were not getting my wolf, too. Sebastian was innocently smiling, listening to the girls, unaware of the male-hungry females they truly were.

I went from worried to jealous so fast that my mind spun with confusion. Feeling insecure over Sebastian had never happened to me before. Then I went to feeling shame because I should be happy for Sebastian making new friends. But the way the two tramps—I mean, nice young ladies—were hanging onto him, clearly not looking for friendship, had me back to being jealous, and mumbling some inappropriate name calling.

Complete. Emotional. Whiplash.

Images of girls kissing Sebastian violently twisted my stomach, distracting me from noticing Sebastian's body language. Once I focused, I realized Sebastian's smile now looked strained, his eyes were wincing, and he was no longer enjoying the girls' company in the slightest. The girls were oblivious to the signs that were perfectly readable to me.

Before I could worry about why he was irritated—or allow my body to torture me with more jealous tummy aches—his eyes closed. When they opened, they were glassed over, and I knew exactly which Sebastian was appearing. His jaw tightened, and the girls were shed and abandoned.

This version of Sebastian walked toward me like the predatory animal that lurked somewhere in his human form. Before I could react, I was in an aggressive embrace. "Something's wrong," said Sebastian, with a deep voice I had not heard before.

It was almost… seductive.

I felt a sudden unexpected shiver in parts of my body that had yet to react to the male gender. Sebastian let out a moan. He whispered, "What did you just do? It's making it worse."

His whisper in my ear caused me another shiver.

Sebastian's body pressed to mine. "Oh, God. You did it again."

My mind struggled to comprehend what was happening to us.

"Your scent… it's…" Sebastian let out a rumble during the word, "*changing*."

I was becoming breathy as my body became more and more stimulated.

"*Oh, shit.*" I wasn't sure if I said that because of how his rumble affected me, causing another shiver, or because we, indeed, were slipping into deep shit—metaphorically, of course.

New Sebastian continued to speak as his body slowly forced mine backward. "I thought the surprise of me being here would be great, but something is happening inside me, and I think I'm losing control in a *very* good way."

I was so engrossed in what he had to say and how his body was helping him say it that I didn't realize Sebastian was trapping me in a corner between a wall and the end of a row of lockers. He nuzzled along my neck. His shoulders hunched over me, giving us privacy.

There was no controlling the next shiver, and I began not to want to. And I was never so thankful that teenagers rush to the cafeteria at lunchtime, emptying the halls in a hurry.

The wonder and awe in Sebastian's voice that usually had me pondering in deep thought were gone. Now, he sounded and felt dominating and had me contemplating something else altogether.

"Marley." He began to move his body against mine. "You know how I don't like Jimmy's scent on you?"

I nodded, but I wasn't really comprehending his words at this point. My eyes shut of their own accord, simply reacting to the effects his domineering rubbing was having on my body. Something raged inside Sebastian, a call of sorts, and my body was willingly answering.

"When he put his arm around you, I-I almost *bit* him."

I suddenly froze, listening to that part of my brain that was screaming for me to get a grip and hear the possible severity of the situation. Sebastian, on the other hand, was slipping deeper into his trance, brushing his face on my neck.

"And now, smelling him on you is making me very, *very angry*." He tightened his hold on me. "I'm feeling extra strong. And whatever is happening inside you is stirring my insides into action."

"Oh, Sebastian… I think we're in trouble."

"No trouble. I could take on the world right now, but I must touch you first." His body pushed into mine. Another ripple of shivers rushed through me, and another moan came from Sebastian.

This was escalating at a rapid rate. "Sebastian, I need you to try to focus."

He slowly licked my neck. "I am focused."

Shivers. "Uh, silky tongue is not helping me. Listen," I tried to whisper, "I think your harmless rubbing me at home just kicked into not-so-harmless hormones, and I think Romy is staking his claim—for real this time. And—I'm not exactly fighting this—*new* you—which is making for a catastrophic—"

Another lick.

Another shiver.

Another moan.

My head leaned back against the wall to give him more access. "Oh, that feels so good—*no*. Damn! I gotta get you out of here and us both into a *very* cold shower."

His teeth grazed my neck when I tried to push him away. He quietly growled. "I can't stop. I hate his smell on you and will replace it. Now." A shadow of Romy flashed.

My wolf was about to have a territorial breakdown in my school hallway. "Sebastian, you *must* listen to me. I'm going to hold your hand and lead you out the front door—ow!"

He *bit* me!

My shoulder didn't hurt, but the sudden nibble he delivered shocked the hell out of Sebastian. His words sounded refocused. "Don't move, Marley. I'm so sorry. M-my need to dominate you is making me hostile inside." The tremble that vibrated through his body told me how hard he was struggling for control over himself.

Now I was scared, not for *my* safety, but for any male who dared approach me. Somehow, I had to convince *Romy* he was in control of me so Sebastian could calm down. So I did something I had never done before. I licked Sebastian's neck the way he had licked mine. As soon as my tongue touched his skin, his eyes rolled back into his head, and he released a guttural growl.

Since I clearly had his attention, I whispered, "No one will touch me, Romy... only you, and I won't leave your side." Then, remembering the TV program on wolves, I tried to show my submission by exposing the side of my neck and lowering my eyes.

His grip loosened.

Putting my arms around his neck and looking over his shoulder, I noticed we were alone and took a deep breath as my body began to relax a little. The need to rush Sebastian home wasn't as immediate.

With his lips to my exposed neck, Sebastian's voice returned. "Marley, w-what's happening to me?"

I hated hearing his desperation. My arms tightened around him. "Shhh. You're okay. I'm here. I love you. I'm here." After I said the words, I began to wonder where the word *love* really stood with us now. Sebastian and I had spoken about love being at different levels. I'd thought, as friends, we had been at the deepest. And now? Well, I didn't know where we stood. "Sebastian, do you think you consider me part of your... *pack,* or something?"

His eyes finally came out of hiding and looked into mine. "You *are* my pack, Marley."

My heart bled for him. "Oh, Sebastian." For the first time I wondered if I had made a mistake. I whispered, "Should I have left you in the cave all those years ago? Have I ruined you?"

His hands grasped my face, forcing my arms to drop. "I followed *you,* remember? I always will, Marley. I'm here, aren't I?"

My lips kissed his palm. "How *are* you here?"

He watched his thumb caress my bottom lip as he spoke. "I researched and made phony transcripts. I figured I would be gone before they figured it out."

I gently kissed his thumb, until I realized what he had said. My chest tightened. "Gone?"

"School's over in May, but after what just happened, I think I'll leave and not come back."

"Are you leaving me, Sebastian?" I clung to him.

When his expression changed to a gentle one, I knew he understood me. "No, my Marley. I want to live with you. I will only go if you ask me to. Are you asking me to?"

I wanted the opposite. I wanted his lips on mine with promises of never leaving. "No."

He kept staring at my mouth. "I told you: forever, Marley. I will never lie to you."

His words rocked my soul. With everything we had been through and experienced together, I couldn't believe I was realizing I wanted to take a monumental step with my wolf. As recognition of my feelings came barreling forward, I learned I was in love with my best friend.

"Let's take a long walk home and talk, okay?" I quietly said to Sebastian.

When he started growling, I was confused until I heard "There you are!" Jimmy was teasingly judging me. "Mar-cakes, what are you and Boy Toy up to?"

Our escape from school had just gotten delayed and complicated.

"Shh!" I whispered to Romy, whose tensing body told me he was partially losing control again. Then I not-so-easily switched spots with Sebastian and put my back to his front in an attempt to hold him there. Sebastian's hands immediately went to my hips, pulling me to him. Chills broke out all over my body. His moaning response vibrated on my back.

"Ready to eat?" Jimmy asked.

"Uh…"

"Not a trick question, girl."

"Uh…"

A low voice answered from behind me. "Lunch sounds good."

Jimmy walked away, laughing. "Then you *clearly* haven't heard Marlena bitch about our food here. I'll save a spot in line for the lovebirds."

I couldn't move. I didn't know what to do. Sebastian whispered in my ear. "I'm so sorry, Marley. I was too excited to be in school with you to think this all through."

I pulled one of his hands from my hip and kissed it. "Never apologize for your beautiful heart's actions." I turned to him. "Sebastian, you must stay in control. If anyone gets a glimpse or suspects—"

"I know. I'll become a science project for the government or the highest bidder." He tried to smile, but the thought of him being like that poor alien—a lab rat—made my knees try to falter. I rushed my arms around his waist. "That would kill me."

A kiss landed on the top of my head. "Can I hold your hand in there? I think it will help."

Denying Sebastian or Romy *anything* was like denying my soul life.

Entering the cafeteria promised the rumor mill would go into overdrive again, but what choice did I have? Skipping school with the new student would surely get back to my parents, which would start more trouble than what could transpire here—hopefully.

When Sebastian and I joined Jimmy in line, he chuckled. "T's gonna flip."

Trevor was already sitting with his harem.

"Why do you say that?" I asked.

"New guy was not part of his Get Marlena Jealous plan."

My jaw dropped. "What?"

Sebastian was right. Trevor was trying to control me with his actions. My heart raced with what this meant. I thought Trevor had moved on, but now I knew my holding Sebastian's hand was going to trigger a reaction. And with Romy lurking, I was becoming alarmed at the possibility of conflict between the two alphas.

Pulling cash from my back pocket, I whispered to Sebastian, "Just follow my lead." I discreetly stuck the money in his front pocket. "This is to pay for your lunch."

We reached the servers, and I grabbed two lunch trays, slid one to Sebastian, and proceeded to pick out what I thought Romy would like best. Sebastian hadn't said a word. He watched and grabbed what I did and followed me to the register. My lunches were free because my parents were poor and needed assistance. Sebastian paid cash, and we headed for the table. Jimmy led us, with a shit-eating grin on his face.

Trevor looked up and high-fived his buddy. "Hound, my man, ya found her?"

"And company," Jimmy mumbled to me as he sat across from Trevor.

Trevor looked behind me and froze.

This wasn't a good sign.

Acting casual, I said, "Trevor, this is Sebastian. He's new." I set down my tray and sat next to Jimmy.

Sebastian sat at my other side. "Nice to meet you."

It had to be weird to say that to someone he had known since my first day of school.

Trevor said nothing, ate nothing, just stared at Sebastian and me. Our other acquaintances, including the girls hanging on Trevor, watched him watching us. Sebastian's tremors told me Romy understood that Trevor still wanted me. Under the table, I rested my hand on Sebastian's thigh to try and soothe his animalistic needs. He looked at me with worried eyes that brutally yanked on my heartstrings. I couldn't say it out loud, so my eyes whispered back, *Shhh, you're okay. I love you.*

I jumped as a tray roughly slid into mine. Trevor walked away.

Under his breath, Jimmy said, "I'll go talk to him," and left our table.

I just tried to breathe and get much-needed oxygen to my nervous lungs.

Releasing Sebastian's hand and leaving him at his next class made me extremely anxious. My body and heart didn't want to leave him. I rubbed my chest, trying to calm down my worry for him. *What if something triggers Romy? What if security is called in, and Sebastian is hauled away without me knowing it? He will be alone!*

I shouldn't have been, but I was shocked to see Trevor waiting by my locker. I stopped walking and stood in the hallway, searching Trevor's face, as students passed me, talking about things that seemed so trivial. His expression showed confusion and hurt. I wondered if I owed him an apology. Even with what Trevor did after our break-up and how quickly he did it, I felt disloyal to him. As every moment passed that day, I realized more and more that I had loved Sebastian the way a girl loves a boy ever since Sebastian became one. I chose him over Trevor, and that was while Sebastian was still only Romy. Now that Romy was also Sebastian, I saw that Trevor never had a chance.

Trevor waited patiently for me to approach him, even as the bell rang, announcing we were now late to class. The only word he said was, "When?"

I opened my locker without looking at him. "When what, Trevor?"

His voice sounded raspy. "When did you start with him?"

I grabbed my book for my next class, closed my locker, and leaned my shoulder against it for support. "Since I met him."

Trevor winced for a moment. "When was that?"

I felt more guilt and tried to be kind. "Really want to know?"

He swallowed hard and looked down. "Probably not."

"I never cheated on you." I needed him to know that.

Trevor nodded but wouldn't look at me. "I believe you. Funny, I guess. I was always jealous of Romy. Little did I know there was someone else." He inhaled deeply. "I never cheated on you either, Marlena. I know I've been an ass here lately, but—guess it don't matter now."

"No, it doesn't," I told him as gently as I could.

"It's the way you look at him," Trevor said so quietly I could barely hear him.

"What do you mean?"

I never thought the day would come when I would see Trevor be emotional, but there I was, watching his eyes well up as we stood in the empty hallway. He swallowed again. "In the cafeteria, the way you looked at him... that's how I knew I'd lost you."

Those words told me our break-up was not our goodbye—this was.

He finally looked at me, as if to confirm the words bringing him pain. There was nothing I could say to change the truth. "I'm sorry."

Trevor, king of the playground, lost hold of his emotions for a few seconds. Then he caught his breath. "I'm going to miss you, Marlena."

Even though we would see each other every day, I knew what he meant. Nothing between us would ever be the same. Tears fell from my eyes as my heart not only forgave him, but appreciated what he was giving to me at this very moment. A true gift was being delivered to the wounds in my heart. I learned that Trevor *was* the guy I had always believed him to be. The asshole cover that I had seen recently was just an act.

"I'll miss you, too."

The last tears I would ever see come from Trevor's eyes slid down his cheek as his hands gently captured my face. He spoke out choked words. "Goodbye, Marlena." He kissed my lips. I knew Romy was going to have a fit, but I needed that kiss. I needed that goodbye and peace in my heart, so I took it.

The simple, meaningful kiss ended. I touched his face. "Goodbye, T."

He chuckled, leaning his forehead to mine. "You always know how to make me laugh."

I grinned. "Some things will never change?"

He released me and wiped his eyes. "I hope not, girl." He stopped and looked at me with a big smile.

I giggled. "Now what?"

"You made me into a damn a country song!"

"What?" I laughed.

He walked away, laughing and singing "The One That Got Away", a song by Jake Owens. Maybe not the most cheerful song, but my lifelong friend was smiling. I knew he would be just fine.

CHAPTER TEN

MAGIC AND MORE

"**M**ARLEY!"

Sebastian looked so much better after his class and excited to see me. The two Battered and Tattered Ts that were clinging to each of his arms were shed *again*, and he ran to me. My feet didn't ask or wait for my brain's command. They took off running to Sebastian. When our bodies slammed together, my eyes closed. It felt as though his soul was comforting mine. I think it was. I think it always will.

I consumed every rub and coo his face offered until he froze. A growl escaped my Sebastian, notifying me that Romy wanted to be heard. I could have been scared, but I was too happy. What Trevor had done for me, even though it annoyed Romy, had me on such a high that I felt *free*. I laughed at Sebastian preparing to throw a fit and I kissed him.

I had kissed my best friend many times, but not on the lips, and not like this. The sensation was so shocking to us both that we neither would nor could shut our eyes. While I held my lips to his, Sebastian's face went from anger to wonderment. His full lips were so soft and wonderful to feel, I wasn't sure I would ever find the strength to pull away. Sebastian was no longer worrying about scents on me as he pulled me closer, his large hands flat on my back.

Since the hallway had many students passing us and staring, I finally withdrew my lips from Sebastian's. He rapidly inhaled. "I'm feeling something, Marley." I stood in front of him, mirroring him, nodding in absolute amazement. His hand clutched his chest. "Marley, my heart's pounding. Why?"

The warning bell rang. Neither of us moved.

"I-I have to go." I was pleasantly enlightened to see my kiss affect him so. He nodded and slowly backed away from me. Since he seemed to be as much in a trance as I was, I was shocked when he turned, grabbed, a girl and... kissed her.

I squealed. "What are you doing?"

He released her—and her confused expression—then looked at me and smiled. Walking backward, he answered, "Experiment! Seeing if all kisses can make my heart thump."

I smiled, shaking my head in disbelief. "And the discovery?"

He looked excited. "Marley is the only one with *magic* kisses."

My hands flew over my inflamed, blushing face, as my peers looked to see who gave out *magical* kisses.

As we walked to the bus, Sebastian's smile was undeniable. I was electrified with the hope he was smiling for the same reason I was—the *kiss*.

Sebastian leaned down to whisper in my ear. "I urinated in a urinal today."

Nope, he was not smiling for the same reason.

I struggled for words. "Umm, how exciting? Good boy?"

Sebastian stood up straight and proudly walked. "Thank you. It was... *liberating*."

I rolled my eyes. "Can only imagine, Wolf Boy."

At the bus, the happy moment shriveled, and reality struck me hard. *How can I have Sebastian on the bus with me? Where would he get dropped off? Will he be okay?* I was sure I was going to hyperventilate with worry.

"See you at home?" Sebastian whispered.

Pulled out of my thoughts, I faced him. "How will you get there?"

His smile was full of confidence. "The same way I got here." He spoke as though my need to worry about his transportation was unjustified. Seeing I wasn't satisfied, Sebastian added, "I have followed your bus several times to see the best way to get here and the layout of your school—to learn more about buildings and structures." He pointed over his shoulder to my school.

Looking at the mountains and woods, it was easy to see how he had stayed hidden but close enough to gather input for his surprise. His *surprise* spooked me again, and I panicked, grasping his hand.

Before I could say a word, he asked, "Can I have some more magic?"

For the second time that day, my cheeks set fire, and I became so bashful it was probably nauseating to anyone witnessing it. I nodded like the shy schoolgirl I was becoming. Everything went silent as his lips came for mine. I could only hear his breath and mine. As soon as our lips met, the same tummy tingle rushed back to me, stealing my breath.

Sebastian was right and wrong about our kisses. They were definitely magical, but it was because of *his* magic, not mine.

As I got on the bus, catcalls were shouted, and my mortification began. Jimmy mocked me. "I *do* know him, Jimmy."

Trevor sang, "The one that got away…"

They both loved my humiliation. It was nice. It felt right to sit on the bus and be teased and toyed with. It felt as if old times were coming back and that my friends and I had not missed a beat. I wasn't even bothered when another girl sat in Trevor's lap. Parts of my world were coming full circle, while others were just opening up.

All the way home, I thought and planned how to fit both Romy and Sebastian into my life, now that Sebastian was becoming part of the general population. I also thought about what kept making my belly quiver: the kiss. Never would I have imagined kissing one boy could be so unlike kissing another, but my feelings for Sebastian seemed to compound with every touch, and I could only imagine what it would be like for us to experience a more extensive moment.

The bus pulled up, and Trevor playfully said, "Ol' Faithful."

My head jerked up. *It can't be!*

Romy sat at my bus stop, waiting for me with his tongue hanging out as he panted. All the stops unloading the students had given Romy a head start. I ran off the bus to greet him, as if I hadn't just kissed him forty-five minutes earlier.

Anxious to talk to Sebastian, I ran inside and told my mom I was spending time with Romy in the woods. She was in the kitchen, of course, and no questions were asked. She looked at Romy from the sink as he greeted her with a nuzzle. "There you are. Haven't seen you all day."

His tail wagged and wagged for her. *He missed my mom.* Of course he had. She was who he was with whenever I was at school. I placed my hand on my chest, sighing. Romy sat in front of me, waiting.

"Be back in time for dinner," Mom called out as Romy and I left.

I ran with a wolf nipping at my heels, teasing, playing with me. Yelping in excitement, I picked up my speed. Once out of sight and near hidden clothes in a tree, Sebastian appeared, smiling. As he reached up to a branch to gather what was stored in a plastic bag, he asked, "Magic?" He pulled on some jeans, waiting for my response.

I laughed, realizing Sebastian was a *true* male at heart. "No, no magic 'til we talk."

He stuck his tongue out at me and sat down on a big boulder.

I paced in front of him. "What were you doing at my school?"

He smirked. "Didn't we go over this? I'll follow you anywhere."

I stomped my foot and tapped frustrated toes. "How am I supposed to argue with that?"

He leaned back onto his elbows, looking as if he were being served on a platter. "You're not, Marley. Just take time to reflect and know how much I love you."

Yes, my knees went weak, *again.*

"Sebastian, stop that!"

He sat up, alarmed. "What did I do?"

I told the sky above me, "He doesn't even understand!"

"What do I not understand?" He rushed to me. "Marley, I thought we were playing around."

"We are, but I'm worried, and I'm trying to be serious. We need to discuss things like my parents and people now having seen you, a-and it is soooo hard with you looking like that."

His arms came around my waist. His expression was full of concern. "What am I looking like?"

"Like, like something making me want… more!" I almost yelled.

A war was being waged inside my body. On one side of the battlefield was my heart, worrying for my best friend. The opposing side was full of hormones, demanding to be released to conquer the beautiful young man holding me. I was intensely aware of every touch he offered, whether on purpose or not. His bare chest brushing my clothed breast had never captured my attention before, but now, each of his moves had all my focus. Sebastian's hand rested on my cheek, heightening my desire for his kiss.

"More?" His eyebrows furrowed.

Nestling my face into his palm, I struggled to voice my needs. "I want… I want… Yes, more."

"Tell me what more means, and I will give it to you."

The same hormones ran and celebrated with victory flags as they sensed my surrender. I looked into his eyes and sounded as if I were begging. "Magic."

I think I *was* begging.

Shiver.

Sebastian's body stiffened as a revelation crossed his face. A sudden flash of insecurity spoke to my ego when it occurred to me Sebastian might not want me the same way I wanted him. I tried to retreat, but his arm tightened around my waist, pulling my body against his. The contact caused another wave, but this one was even stronger.

His eyes closed as his mouth opened, exposing the softness inside I wanted to taste.

Shiver.

Sebastian moaned as his hand tightened on my face. Not opening his eyes, Sebastian seemed to be tuning himself to every electrical pop and sizzle that my body experienced. He groaned, "Marley," and opened his eyes to show me a hunger matched by no one who had looked at me before.

Shiver.

Another groan.

His hand slid to the nape of my neck, and his fingers tangled in my hair, taking hold of me, positioning me for what he intended to do next. My desire elevated as his eyes fell to my lips. My breathing became impossible to control as he panted with need and an excitement that left me helplessly at his mercy.

With his luscious lips parted, Sebastian leaned to me and took my upper lip between his. I whimpered. I shook with want as my lips closed around his bottom lip. Never could I have guessed that something so gentle could be so sensual. His eyes closed as his lips drew mine in. His eyes squeezed shut. He captured my bottom lip. With every caress of lips, our breaths mingled and created an intimate warmth that I felt down to my toes.

He whispered my name while we both experienced exquisite new sensations.

When his tongue slowly and tentatively entered my mouth, I thought my world would end because my heart was going to explode with need. But his tongue touched mine, and I realized my world was *not* going to end. It was just beginning.

CHAPTER ELEVEN

BLISSFUL IGNORANCE AND LIES

LYING IN THE DARK WITH Sebastian had become an every-night event, but it wasn't innocent any longer. The part of me that was becoming a woman craved the man who held me. Our special friendship was now partly desire, infused with the love of a lifetime.

Love of a lifetime.

I was astonished by the leap I took that day. How effortless it felt to see Sebastian as mine forever. No words had been spoken to label what we had become, and Sebastian had asked no questions. What was transpiring between us was so natural that I lay in that bed, wishing every young woman could experience such a liberating event. To know someone is truly committed to you is to have the sensation of another soul blending perfectly with yours.

His fingers drifted up and down my arm. "Do you remember when I told you about why I believe in God?"

"Yes, you felt something around you. You never felt alone."

After a quiet moment, Sebastian softly said, "I believe you are a part of God."

My throat tightened with the incredible words.

"Even when I'm not with you, Marley, I feel you all around me."

My eyes closed as his love soared through me.

"Marley, I believe moments like this... emotions like this... they're what God wants for all of us, all his creatures. I thought your kisses were magic. but now I know it's you. It's you, Marley. *You* are magic to me."

A tear slid down my cheek to rest on the pillow we shared.

Entranced with the love I felt for Sebastian, I was blissfully unaware of all the danger surrounding us. My age and innocence made it so that the cruel world lurking over our shoulders could not be felt as the magic Sebastian spoke of circled the two of us in a frenzy. I didn't care about his illegal paperwork sitting in the school office, waiting to be discovered. I didn't care that students stared at Sebastian and me as if we were aliens. I didn't comprehend that time was not on our side.

"Anything to tell me, Marlena?" my father asked at the dinner table.

I shrugged. "Don't think so."

Mom's lips pursed. "We want to meet him."

My body jolted. They had already heard about Sebastian. "Umm, okay."

"Where did you meet him?" Dad asked.

Lying to my parents was more difficult than I had suspected it would be. "Uh, at the store. Mom sent me for some things."

"When?" he asked.

"Recently."

"What's his name?" Mom asked in a stern voice.

"Sebastian."

"Where does he live?" I was surprised to hear my father's irritation.

"Over by the apple orchards somewhere."

Mom's eyebrow rose. "Ever been there?"

"No, ma'am."

"How serious is this?" Dad inquired.

"I-I like him."

"Why haven't we met him?"

I looked at my dad. "I didn't want people to think I was just trying to get over Trevor."

His shoulders softened. "Little girl, I know that was hard on you, but I wouldn't think you capable of using a young man to get over another."

After a quiet moment passed, my mom picked up her fork. "Can we have him over for dinner?"

I wanted to say that he was already there, sitting on the floor right next to me. "He wants to meet you. I've been the one holding back."

I knew my dad would appreciate a young man trying to be proper. "I like hearing that. Shows he has good character." He began to eat again.

"Maybe we shouldn't have Romy inside when Sebastian comes over," my mom suggested.

My father nodded. "I agree. Don't need this young kid getting bit by a jealous wolf."

I was stunned. I hadn't thought about that detail either, but was grateful my parents had already solved the problem, for now. "Uh, okay. I'll put Romy outside before Sebastian comes over." I poked at my plate. "He's a great guy. I think you both will like him."

They did.

Sebastian knocked on the front door that weekend, saying his father had just dropped him off. It was awkward, but Sebastian acted as if he had never been in this home and had not been living with the parents he was supposedly meeting for the first time. Maybe knowing my parents so well was how he knew what to say, how to act, and how to have my parents fall head over heels for him. Or maybe Sebastian was just being himself, and that was enough for anyone to think highly of him.

Sitting at our table in the kitchen was a little confusing. It was normally Romy sitting next to me on the floor. Now, it was Sebastian in a chair with my parents.

My dad asked, "Who are your parents, Sebastian?"

"No one we know," I said in a nervous hurry. "They moved here recently."

My father nodded and dropped that subject but was right on to the next. "So you wish to date my daughter, young man?"

I cringed in embarrassment, but Sebastian's face lit up. "Yes, sir. She's so willing to explore and learn."

Needless to say, my dad's shoulders bunched up, and his face looked alarmed with what I might be *taught* by my suitor.

I mumbled to Sebastian, "Clarify *what* I'm willing to explore."

Clueless about what his words had insinuated, Sebastian enthusiastically added, "Where to begin?"

My dad went pale.

"God and responsibilities—"

"Responsibilities?" Mom asked.

Sebastian leaned forward, exuding passion. "Yes. Our everyday actions can affect the ones we care for. So always respect and cherish someone's well-being."

My parents looked at each other with wide eyes.

"Marley's view on the world not only impresses me—humbles me—but it makes me want to be a better man."

Yes, it was cheesy. It was definitely over the top, but when said with such sincerity, anyone who heard Sebastian's words knew he meant each one. My parent's lips slowly turned up, and my suitor was as welcome as could be.

At the end of the extremely successful evening, Sebastian lied again, saying his father was coming to pick him up, and left out the front door.

Dad exhaled deeply. "I really like him, Amelia."

My mom was headed to the back door. "Me, too! He felt so familiar to me, and *wow,* does he have it bad for our daughter, Everett." She opened the door and sang out, "Romy!" She turned back to us. "That's whose eyes Sebastian has. Romy's." She mumbled, "How's *that* for a coincidence?"

A beautiful gray wolf came running across the yard, wagging his tail. I knelt and opened my arms. Romy happily nuzzled me. "Missed you, my Romy."

My mother and father had asked Sebastian to come back the next night. I assumed we were in for another great evening, but we were off to a rocky start. Sebastian walked through the front door and shook my dad's hand.

He studied Sebastian and said, "I used to have a shirt just like that."

Sebastian and I were two deer caught in headlights. I couldn't believe how careless I had gotten.

My mom graciously said, "There is no shame in shopping at the thrift shop."

Dad patted Sebastian's shoulder. "Of course not. A man too proud to do so is a man who has questionable character values." He laughed. "I guess my shirt wanted to come home!"

My mom joined in his laughter while Sebastian and I attempted to join but sounded more like nervous hyenas. As we sat on the couch and chairs, I figured the night couldn't get worse.

"I feel like I know you, Sebastian," said my mom, looking at him adoringly.

Sebastian smiled as if recognizing her love. "Maybe because I already feel at home. You both have been so welcoming to me. Thank you for that. I was nervous."

My dad laughed. "When I met Amelia's dad, I thought I was going to shit my pants."

"Everett!" my mom hollered in embarrassment.

"What?"

Sebastian laughing with my parents was an out-of-body experience for me. I watched them interact, feeling my life had blended into my dream. Fear of this moment had melted away, and hope had taken its place. I allowed myself to fantasize about Sebastian and me having a place of our own someday and us coming to my parents' house for holiday dinners.

Before I knew it, two weeks had passed, and Sebastian had become the son they never had. My ignorant bliss continued.

Had I only known what damage lies could cause.

I hadn't been sleeping more than a few hours when I woke to Sebastian. He was sleeping behind me, but his snuggling was different. Sebastian had his hands on my hips, pulling my rump into his front, and a certain body part of Sebastian's was a tad bit... excited. Not being completely ignorant of sex, I quickly assumed that he must be having an interesting dream. I giggled. "Sebastian."

He said nothing, just kept pulling me to him.

I whispered louder, "Sebastian?"

Completely unaware of what he had been doing, Sebastian groggily snuggled closer to me and sweetly asked, "Are you okay?"

I couldn't stop grinning as I looked over my shoulder to see his face. "Yes. Are you?"

His eyes opened, and he looked confused. "I think so. Why?"

My chuckle was barely containable. "Umm, you have... new... growth."

"Growth?"

I rolled over to face him, giggling, and then I pointed to his private area. Still perplexed, Sebastian looked to where I had pointed. He only had boxers on, so it was clear. Sebastian was having his first erection. His eyes popped out of his head. "What's wrong with me?"

I touched his chest, still smiling. "Too bad my parents don't pay for Cinemax. I heard their late-night shows could sum this up for you. Sebastian, you know how you've been changing inside? Becoming a little more *possessive* of me with scents?"

He nodded but was not smiling. I think he believed he was dying.

"Well, that inside change is now becoming evident, on the outside."

"Marley, what does this mean?" Sebastian practically gasped.

"Shh, you're okay. This is very normal for guys."

He took a relieved breath but motioned his hand for more of an explanation.

I shook my head in disbelief. "I guess I'm all you've got as a teacher. Okay, umm, remember when we saw that couple kissing on TV?" He nodded. "Well, sometimes kissing leads to touching—"

Before I could say more, Sebastian interrupted, "Why?"

"Uh, because it's supposed to feel good—bring you pleasure."

"Have you been touched?"

"Er, uh, only a little. Anyway, your girlfriend or companion can touch you, or you can touch yourself."

He pointed to his new acquaintance. "Here?"

"Yes." I confirmed. He reached down to begin experimenting. I whisper-screamed, "Not now!"

Sebastian stopped. "I thought you said it will bring me pleasure."

"Yes, but I'm here."

"I know."

"I don't think I should watch you—you—uh, bring yourself to climax."

"Climax?"

"Sweet Jesus, why me?" I asked myself, then answered Sebastian, "Yes, climax, orgasm. Once your private area"—I awkwardly pointed again—"down there gets really happy, it produces stuff to make babies."

"Reproduction."

"Yes! Reproduction," I said as softly as possible.

"Does *that* feel good, too?"

I shrugged. "Some say so. I personally wouldn't know."

He smiled eagerly. "Let's try it."

"Easy there, Wolf Boy. We are not quite ready for all that. We just started the kissing part."

Sebastian looked happy. "Okay, you said touching is next. Show me how."

My jaw dropped. "What? Listen, sometimes you say things that are... umm... questionable, especially to other people."

"Oh. If I do this again, will you tell me?"

"Yes, and then you can cover it up by saying 'Gotcha.'"

"Got-cha?"

"Yes. Gotcha," I teased, trying to cover up what I was truly thinking about, about how much I really *wanted* to touch him—to know what he felt like down there, but my parents were downstairs sleeping. It just didn't feel right. Biting my bottom lip, I stayed quiet.

"Marley?"

I refocused. "Uh, yeah. Tell you what... my parents are leaving for a couple of days over spring break. Why don't we... experiment then?"

His greedy smile was his answer.

The next couple of nights were full of desperate kisses and anticipation of alone time.

"Are you sure you'll be okay?" My mom stood with a packed bag in her hand.

My dad kissed my cheek. "Amelia, only a madman would break into this house with a two-hundred-pound wolf standing guard." He chuckled as he took her bag and headed out the front door.

My mom knelt in front of Romy. "You'd probably die for her. Wouldn't you, Romy?"

She received two barks and a lick across the face.

My mom stood, smiling. "If he just licked his butt, I'm going to shower."

One bark. No butt licking.

Worried arms circled me again.

"Mom, I'm a big girl. Go! Have a great time."

"Okay, but we will be three hours away, so if you need to, call Sebastian, and we will rush home." She headed for the door then turned back and whispered, "Don't tell your father I said that. He may love that boy, but, well, he's a dad, and you're his little girl." Then she was out the front door.

I loudly exhaled. "Didn't think they were ever going to leave."

I watched my dad's truck exit the driveway. Romy ran up the stairs. I knew he was as excited as I was. We were having alone time to take another step in the physical spectrum of our relationship.

Within moments, Sebastian trotted down the steps in only jeans. My heart began to pound as shivers caused havoc in the body while I rushed to Sebastian. He had a sinister grin as he approached me. My arms greedily opened, wanting anything he had to offer. Lips crushed to mine as his arms aggressively pulled me to him. I was delighted as our tongues began to battle with a ravishing hunger—

Ring!

Struggling for air, Sebastian and I both suspiciously looked at the kitchen phone ringing on the wall. My parents were gone, and their few friends knew this. Sebastian's arms tightened around me as he begged, "Please don't answer that."

We started hungrily kissing again, but then I worried. "It could be important."

In between kisses, Sebastian said, "You know who it is."

Keeping our lips connected, I walked backward toward the phone. "It's Friday night. T and Hound are *busy*."

"I want to be busy," Sebastian growled.

Shiver.

Moan.

I leaned back and answered the phone. "Hello?"

Sebastian groaned again, but this time it wasn't the happy kind.

"Your parents gone?" Trevor asked.

"Uh, yeah," I answered with much confusion.

"Good. Me and Hound are coming over."

"Wait—"

Click.

A not-so-happy Sebastian glared at me.

As innocently as possible, I shrugged. "You were right?"

With determination, Sebastian began kissing me again. "I need you, Marley."

My body yearned for his as we kept talking through needy kisses. "We can kiss 'til they get here, then I'll tell them to leave."

"I refuse to be Romy tonight."

I was devouring him. "I know. Just you and me."

Sebastian and I became so consumed with the freedom we were experiencing that I hadn't realized we'd backed ourselves to the couch. My knees bent, and Sebastian's body, more than willing, followed mine. With not enough room for both of us, Sebastian was forced to lie on top of me. I felt Sebastian having a repeat performance of the other night.

Sebastian froze. "Marley?"

"It's okay. It's normal, remember?" I tried to soothe him. "Shh... relax and kiss me."

Sebastian's next kiss started off hesitantly but slowly deepened as his body released its tension and melted into mine. It is remarkable how your body knows what to do when it is truly aroused by delicious kissing. Sebastian and I were completely immersed in the heat of the moment, allowing our bodies to move against one another. I had experienced Trevor moving his body against mine before, but my body had never responded. With Sebastian, I felt a deep ache, pleading for more of him as my hips moved involuntarily.

Our pants and grunts were rhythmically in unison until Sebastian threw his face into my neck, struggling terribly. "Oh, God, they're coming, and we don't want to be interrupted."

In the heat of passion, I repeated, "No, we don't," thinking he was speaking of us.

I heard a vehicle approaching my house, but when my eyes opened, I was scared for Trevor and Jimmy because *we* was not Sebastian and me. It was Sebastian and Romy. The young man on top of me looked up at the window above my head and showed shadows that hinted he was about to transition into Romy, not just flash.

I whispered, "No, no, no," but to no avail. Sebastian bravely fought Romy's appearance while Romy growled at the unwanted visitors outside. I could see Sebastian struggling with all his might. His jaw clenched, and his eyes strained.

That moment was as surreal as it was frightening. I had no choice but to scold the shadow of the hairy version of Sebastian. "Romy! You stop this right now!"

Romy faded away, and Sebastian collapsed on top of me and tiredly whispered, "Thank you."

Muffled by my home's walls, I heard Jimmy laughing and Trevor saying, "Good to hear Romy's still a pain in the ass."

I kissed the side of Sebastian's face and all that I could reach while he rested in the crook of my neck. I quietly told him, "I'll try to get them to leave."

An exhausted Sebastian mumbled, "I don't know why Romy gets this way with you. *I* don't want to be so possessive."

A knock vibrated off the back door, so I whispered, "He's a wolf and is treating me as he would if I were a wolf too." I slid out from under Sebastian and joked, "A wolf he apparently has a major crush on."

Sebastian slowly rolled over, smiling. "I have a crush on you, too."

Walking to the door backward, I almost tripped and fell because I was enamored by the handsomeness on my couch. With needy regret, I opened the door. "Hey, guys. I'm sorry you made the trip for nothing, but I'm laying low tonight."

"Great," Trevor said as he walked right past me, entering my house, not concerned with my annoyance. He suddenly stopped, seemingly surprised to see Sebastian on the couch—shirtless.

"Oh." He grinned at me. "No wonder Romy is misbehaving. I see his jealous trait is still intact."

I was a little shameful but happy that Trevor would now understand why he needed to leave.

"Glad I brought plenty of beer."

Or not.

"Beer? I don't think that's a good idea," I tried to explain.

Jimmy followed Trevor in with another twelve-pack, asking, "Where is Mr. Jealous anyway?"

"Uh," I stuttered. "Uh, put him outside—the front door—just now. Yes, I *just now* put him outside by way of the front door."

I was pretty sure my babble would be questioned but, yet again, I was wrong. Jimmy looked at Sebastian. "Boy Toy! How's it going?" Jimmy stopped in his tracks. "Damn, my friend, do you live at a gym or something?"

I glanced at Sebastian, now standing, inspecting himself, thinking something was wrong, and I admired his incredibly built physique.

Trevor glared at the abs of perfection and mumbled, "They're not *that* defined." He told me, "Don't be ridiculous," summing up all the facts in guy language. "Beer is *always* a good idea. And Marlena! Spring break, baby. Besides, your friend here looks like he could afford a few calories in his diet." He headed to the kitchen. "What do you do, Sebastian, *run* to school every day?"

Sebastian went to open his trap until my eyes warned him not to say, "Yes, as a matter of fact I do." The subject was dropped. And apparently, Sebastian spoke the guy language, because next thing I knew, he was next to me, asking, "Beer?"

Jimmy put beer in my refrigerator, cheering. "Boy Toy!"

Trevor was already handing one to Sebastian, when I said, "Wait!"

Sebastian looked so intrigued. "I've always wondered what Everett drinks every night after work."

Sympathy made me feel guilty about trying to deny Sebastian something he considered a mystery.

Trevor simply looked confused. "How do you know what Marlena's dad does every night?"

"Uh, I told him," I rushed to explain.

Walking into the kitchen, Trevor said to Sebastian, "Are you telling me you've never had a beer?"

Sebastian shook his head no as he sniffed the bottle. Jimmy and Trevor both went motionless, watching Sebastian. I saw Sebastian examine things all the time and didn't realize how odd it looked until that moment.

Jimmy asked, "Uh, Mar-cakes, what's he doing?"

I took Sebastian's bottle from him and opened it, rolling my eyes. "He's just messing with you guys." I handed the bottle back to Sebastian, hissing, "Nobody smells their beer bottle."

Sebastian nodded at me, understanding, and then smiled at T and Hound. "Gotcha!"

My palms slammed to my face. "Oh, dear Lord." I hadn't been serious about that cover we discussed, but Trevor and Jimmy burst out laughing, both talking at the same time.

"Oh my God!"

"You totally had me!"

"I was getting concerned."

Then the two cornballs bumped beer bottles in cheer. "Bottoms up," Trevor said, before taking a big swig of his beer. Jimmy followed suit.

Sebastian looked at the beer in his hand. Then he looked at me.

Of course, Trevor had a comment to share. "What? It's just a beer, not moonshine."

Sebastian asked, "What's moonshine?"

Jimmy spit out his beer mid-swallow and proceeded to choke.

"Where did you find this guy?" Trevor handed me an open beer.

Nervous at the thought of how this night was going to go, I found myself guzzling half of it down. Trevor and Jimmy cheered. Sebastian took a sip of his beer, and his face puckered. "Oh, that's awful!"

"Nectar of the Gods? Boy, what are you talking about?" Trevor said in dismay.

Sebastian lost to his first encounter with peer pressure and was already four beers in when we started playing Jenga, a game Sebastian found extremely entertaining. I only drank two beers because my wolf was a bit of a lightweight, as was I, and I decided to keep an eye on him. After another beer in the middle of *another* game of Jenga, Sebastian all of a sudden took a stumbling step away from the kitchen table and said words I will never forget.

"I must poop now." He headed for the back door.

"Dude, where you going?" Trevor asked as Sebastian prepared to step outside.

"Sebastian, my *bathroom* is back here." I pointed to the bottom-floor restroom.

Sebastian stopped and smiled. "Oh, yes, the *bathroom*." He headed in that direction, stating, "Another new experience." The bathroom door shut.

My eyes closed. *Here we go.*

"Are you sure about this one?" Jimmy toyed with me.

My eyes opened and rolled as I blew out air.

"She's sure," Trevor said. "Just watch her watch him."

Jimmy playfully warned me. "T's still suspicious."

"Hound," Trevor growled at him.

"Wait, what's going on?" I asked.

Trevor took a deep, aggravated breath and then finally told me. "I know we're done—that's not why I'm here." My hand gestured for him to continue. "But, I love you—"

My jaw dropped as my eyes went wide, stopping him.

"No! Not that kind of love—*not my style*. Listen, you've been my friend all my life. And even though you're not with me anymore, that doesn't mean I can just stop caring or worrying about you. You have fallen—*really* fallen, for someone I don't know. *No one* knows. I just need to see you're in good hands."

"And then your boy does weird shit like—well, like, try to *shit* outside," Jimmy added.

My shoulders fell. This was supposed to be a romantic night with Sebastian. Instead, it was turning into a wolf's upset stomach from beer, and a Q and A with my ex and Jimmy.

Trevor's eyes scanned my body language. He sounded remorseful. "Marlena, I'm not trying to put pressure on you." He put his arms around me. "It's just—"

I quickly pulled away. "No, don't touch me. He doesn't like it."

When I realized what I had said and how it must have sounded, I tried to fix it, but my excuses fell on deaf ears. Trevor and Jimmy's stances changed as they looked at each other with angered expressions. I quietly pleaded, "No, you're misunderstanding me. I can't explain this. Please trust me."

When Trevor faced me, his outrage was evident. "Has he hurt you?"

This was getting worse. "What? NO. Far from it."

Jimmy's jaw was clenched shut, so he spoke through his teeth. "Then what is going on?"

I put my face in my hands. "I can't tell you—"

"*Marley.*"

I opened my eyes in time to watch the horror of Sebastian looking violently ill. He was pale, stumbling, and his eyes looked half shut. He reached for the staircase but missed, falling to the ground.

"Sebastian!" I screamed and ran to him.

I rolled him over and pulled his upper body into my lap. Weak eyes looked to me with sorrow. "Marley, I'm so sorry, but... alcohol is poison. No one told me how bad it is for you. I'm so sorry."

Trevor knelt at Sebastian's feet. Jimmy hovered behind him. My hand kept touching Sebastian's face. I couldn't understand why he was apologizing to me when *I* was the one who did not warn him. In fairness, I didn't know alcohol was poison to us—or a wolf—but that didn't ease any of my guilt. "Are you going to be okay?"

His shaking hand reached out and touched my cheek. "Yes... but can't stop." His hand weakly fell to his chest as he looked at the boys. "D-don't be mean to her... she had no choice... but to lie." His eyes closed as his body went limp in my arms.

And then, Sebastian became Romy.

CHAPTER TWELVE

UNCOMFORTABLE CONVERSATIONS AND 'THINGS'

TREVOR JOLTED BACKWARD SO FAST that he knocked Jimmy onto his back. Trevor's body—still wanting to get away from the wolf that had just appeared out of nowhere—crawled back and ended up sitting on Jimmy's face.

"Get off me!" Jimmy yelled as he pushed Trevor from his unfortunate resting place.

Trevor slid off, never moving his eyes from what lay half in my lap on top of shredded jeans. Terrified tears rolled down my face. I touched Romy's ribs and could feel him still breathing. It was like he was just resting—maybe even healing.

I glanced at the exasperated faces and pleaded, "Try to keep your minds open. *Please.* For me, try."

Sitting on the floor, Trevor rested his elbows on his knees, hands covering his gaping mouth, probably trying to wrap his mind around what he was witnessing. Jimmy sat up and just stared in what seemed to be numb shock. I stayed silent. Nothing else needed to be said. Sebastian's secret was out for the very first time.

Time seemed to stand still as pressure and worries compounded and weighed down on my shoulders. My two worlds collided every night when Romy became Sebastian, but it was done privately, safely. Now my two worlds were colliding in front of two young men who might not be able to handle the responsibility of keeping Romy safe.

Trevor looked pale when he spoke the first word. "Romy?"

I wiped my dripping tears off his beautiful fur. "Yes, Romy."

"How?" Trevor asked with a quiet astonishment.

Shakily, I answered with truth. "I don't know."

More silence.

"No one knows, do they?" Jimmy asked, as if understanding my actions more clearly.

"Not a soul," I whispered.

"H-has he always been able to… do this?" Trevor asked.

"No, not till he was eleven."

Jimmy looked astonished. "Romy's eleven *now*. Why does Sebastian look so much older?"

"I don't know. He just went from wolf to man, right in front of me."

Jimmy quickly asked, "In front of you? When? Where?"

"The night *we* couldn't find him. He changed—"

"In the woods." Jimmy still looked to be in shock. "That's why I saw a man's set of footprints and a struggle."

I nodded in shame. I had lied to my friend.

"Wait—what tracks, Hound?" Trevor anxiously asked.

"Remember the next morning, when we searched for them both? That's when I saw a man's tracks. Romy changed *after* we carried him home."

Trevor thought. "So we were right. Romy was purposely taking himself from home but not for being sick."

"Yes," I quietly confirmed.

"Did *you* know it was coming?" Jimmy asked.

I was barely audible. "I figured it out."

Trevor pointed to the unconscious Romy. "Is he going to be okay?"

My shoulders shook. "I don't know."

"Well, we can't call nine-one-one for a wolf." Jimmy stated the obvious. "So let's just let him work the beer out of his system."

With Romy in my lap, there were many questions from Trevor and Jimmy, but they were not running to the cops or government. They weren't threatening to turn Romy over to the authorities. Trevor and Jimmy were being my… friends. My gratitude was shown in every answer I could offer. We spoke about how I met Romy and his parents and the heartache that came with the loss of Mother and Father Wolf. Trevor and Jimmy nodded, listening to how Romy became mine to guard and love. They were surprisingly moved when I spoke of how Sebastian viewed the world we took for granted.

"Marlena, this helps me so much," Trevor told me, letting his head fall forward.

"How?"

He chuckled. "Now I know I'm not crazy to have been jealous of a dog."

His chuckle eased some tension in my heart. "You won't tell anyone?"

Jimmy sounded fearful. "They—whoever—would take him—would dissect him—"

My eyes closed as I began to rock, clutching Romy's head to me. Trevor's arm came around my shoulders. "We won't tell. Look at me." My eyes opened, and he said, "Marlena, that would kill you, and killing you would kill me."

"And me." Jimmy nodded.

Trevor slowly reached out, touching Romy's fur. "But Marlena, you two are in over your heads."

"You can say that again." Jimmy also dared to touch Romy.

I watched their caring touches. "Besides the obvious, what do you mean?"

Trevor sat next to me, bewildered. "Why is he in our school?"

I started rocking again as guilt ripped through me. I cried out in despair, "He says he will follow me anywhere!"

"Jesus, he's in love with her." Jimmy grabbed his mouth as if this knowledge made our predicament even more problematic.

Trevor took hold of my face. "And you're in love with him. He *must* stay hidden. Make him drop out." I nodded as more tears ran down my face. I knew he was right. "Have your parents met… Sebastian?"

"Yes. I said he lived over by the orchards."

"You need to let them in on this secret. Or you must fake a break-up or something. Marlena, people *are* going to figure out he has no parents—"

"'Cause there *is* no home by the apple orchards." Jimmy pointed out another hole in my lie.

"What have I done?"

Trevor let me go and took a deep breath while looking at Romy. "You did what you thought was right, but Marlena, this is not a fantasy world where you can live in the public with him. Too many questions will come out of it."

"Maybe she could move away with him after school?" Jimmy asked Trevor, trying to help me.

Trevor gestured at Romy. "Are you kidding me? Am I the only one staring at a wolf that was a human moments ago? Let's forget what the government will do to him if they find out, but what about Marlena?"

Jimmy nodded. "Poke and prod her *just* for being near him." Then his eyes sprang from their sockets as he pulled his hand from Romy. "Am I going to get prodded?"

"No one is getting prodded!" Trevor spit out. "That's my point. I would be wary to show his human form anywhere outside this house. We must make sure this stays a secret."

"We?" I asked, searching for a glimpse of hope.

Trevor leaned forward and kissed my forehead. "Yes, *we*."

Still holding Romy, I leaned into Trevor's chest, almost collapsing. His arms came around me. "Been alone in this for a long time?"

My body trembled as I released all the emotions I'd had to hide all this time.

Jimmy grabbed my hand. "Not alone anymore."

I whispered my appreciation. "Thank you. Thank you."

Jimmy started a fire in the fireplace because of the dropping temperature. Trevor grabbed blankets and pillows and made us a big bed on the floor. Then we moved Romy, who had yet to wake, so I could stay warm while holding him. The fire crackled in the silence while we stared at the flames. Heads on pillows as our heavy hearts rested.

"Marley?"

Trevor, Jimmy, and I began to stir. Arms tightened around my waist from behind. My body melted to Sebastian's when I knew he was okay. Morning light shone through the windows, lifting the night's emotional fog. I rolled to see my favorite being and touched his face. "You look so much better."

"Is Mar-cakes holding a naked guy?"

Trevor answered, "Good thing her pops is out of town."

Sebastian kissed me like he had missed me. "I think I just needed to heal."

Once showered and refreshed, we all sat at the kitchen table and talked about the situation Sebastian and I had created. Sebastian and I answered more questions.

Jimmy was especially concerned when he learned about Romy not liking his scent on me. "You were gonna *eat* me?"

Sebastian laughed. "No. Bite. Didn't want you touching her. Sorry, couldn't help it."

Jimmy sat back in his chair as if amazed he'd unknowingly escaped death.

Trevor's words the night before and that morning confirmed how delusional I had been. When he explained to Sebastian what could happen to me if he and I were exposed, Sebastian growled. Jimmy scooted his chair away.

Who would ever have thought womanizing T would be the levelheaded one to take charge and help in such a dangerous time? "The way I see it, enjoy these few days alone with each other because it's mandatory that any public affections are over. The *break-up* must take place ASAP. Hopefully, no one will ask too many questions. Jimmy and I will say we saw the *break-up* go down. That should help."

Even though the break-up wasn't real, it still made me sad. The reality of what Sebastian and I could never be crushed me. Trevor's hand lifted my drooping chin. "Marlena, we'll figure something out."

Jimmy whispered to Trevor, "Dude, don't touch her. He may bite you." Then he stood, reaching into his pocket, and shocked me when he tossed two condoms on the table.

Trevor's jaw dropped. "What are you doing? She's a virgin."

"Not after this weekend," Jimmy comically stated.

My cheeks lit up with a shameful blush.

"Take them back, and stop embarrassing her," Trevor demanded.

"What are they?" Sebastian innocently asked.

"Oh, boy," uttered Jimmy.

My hand was crossing the table and grabbing the two condoms, which took me by complete surprise. Jimmy pointed to my full, retracting hand. "Told ya."

"Marlena?" Trevor sounded cautious.

I couldn't look at him while clutching the condoms in my lap. "Please don't be disappointed in me, Trevor."

"What? *No.* Who am I to judge? I-I just want to make sure you're *sure* about this."

"Sure about what?" asked Sebastian.

Jimmy shook his head at Sebastian then stated to Trevor, "We're gonna have to show clueless how to use the condoms."

Trevor looked grossed out. "I'm not *showing* him how to use them."

Still standing, Jimmy shrugged. "Then grab a banana for a quick one-two lesson."

Trevor raised his hands, begging Jimmy to stop. "Can you focus for a second?"

Jimmy leaned toward Trevor, his tone no longer joking. "I am. *You're* the one in denial. She is head over heels for this dude, and we just told her she can't be with him the way she wants to. You *know* it's breaking her heart, so don't be stupid! Mark my words, they're bang'n' soon, and if she were to get pregnant, what do you think would happen to her when she delivers a wolf-boy in the hospital?"

"Reproduction? This is what this is all about?"

Jimmy didn't stop setting Trevor straight. "She is our best friend! And alone!"

Sebastian quickly took my face in his hands. He looked so worried. "Is sex a bad thing? I thought you said we were going to enjoy ourselves experimenting while your parents were gone."

"Boom, there it is." Jimmy sat back down.

After reconnecting his unhinged jaw, Trevor stood up, said, "I'll get the banana," and threw two more condoms on my poor mother's once innocent kitchen table.

Waiting for Trevor to return with the soon-to-be-abused fruit, Jimmy shrugged. "Then maybe someday, you guys can move to some remote forest and... and raise pups together or something."

After a very embarrassing and *detailed* demonstration, Sebastian and I were now knowledgeable in the protection department. I stared at the exploited banana lying on the table and hoped Jimmy and Trevor were done, but it didn't stop there. Jimmy and Trevor were concerned with it being my first time and took it upon themselves to educate us further, explaining to Sebastian the physics on how one *thing* is bigger than the other *thing* and he must take his time entering *things*. My cheeks were so red by this point, I was sure blood vessels were exploding under my skin.

Sebastian? He loved learning *anything* and seemed especially attentive to this humiliating conversation.

Trevor and Jimmy said their goodbyes with lots of jokes and innuendoes, but that was not what made me smile so proudly.

"What?" Trevor asked me at the back door.

"You guys said you wouldn't leave me alone in all this, and you didn't. As embarrassing as it was to sit at the kitchen table during your... *lessons*, I'm thankful and proud to call Hound and T my dear, dear friends. I love you both."

Trevor smiled sincerely and went to hug me, but stopped when he heard Jimmy fake a cough. Jimmy pretended to be looking at something very interesting on the floor while pointing to Sebastian, and mumble-singing, "Will *bite* you."

I laughed, throwing my arms around Trevor's waist. Then I looked up at him. "Thank you. Thank you for everything. I can't explain how much easier this is knowing I have you two on my side."

As I went to hug Jimmy, he raised his arms in the air, trying not to touch me. I squeezed his waist as he told Sebastian, "Look, hands free. *Not* touching her."

Sebastian laughed and shook both their hands, and then Sebastian and I were alone.

With me clearly being exhausted from a long, scary night and an interesting morning, Sebastian put us in bed, insisting I needed a nap. He crawled in behind me. "We have plenty of time to put the lessons to the test. Get some rest, my Marley."

I wanted to argue that we were indeed wasting time but fell asleep before I could get a word out. Weight had been lifted off my shoulders, and my body rejoiced and rested.

When I woke, I rolled over to face Sebastian. He was awake, waiting for me. A quiet moment passed as I thought about my parents coming home in two days and times like this being rare. An ache took root in places that desired to be touched and demanded that I seize this moment. "Until my parents come home, I-I don't want to be away from your side. I need you, Sebastian."

Sebastian's eyes searched my face. No words were used because we both knew enough conversation had taken place. My breath raced as I decided what I wanted. "I need magic."

Sebastian's eyes studied me further, and his lips dipped down to caress mine. An understanding of what we had to sacrifice for his safety echoed through every gentle kiss, through every gentle touch. Everything we did next was gentle, almost as if saying goodbye, even though we would not part.

Loving Sebastian came at a high price on my heart, but I was going to take advantage of every moment that day offered. Things that I had never done before and might not get to do again took place on the bed that had carried me through many dreams and nightmares. Once again, it would support me and carry me as I lived out another dream—before facing another nightmare.

Having endless trust in Sebastian was what allowed me to share tender moments with him, learning our bodies naturally. We effortlessly communicated as our bodies joined, becoming one. That day taught me to share private moments only with my best friend, someone who loved me unconditionally, someone who did and would give everything for me as I was giving it all to him. This is something I hope every girl or woman experiences at such a timeless event in her life.

CHAPTER THIRTEEN

STOLEN MOMENTS

MY PARENTS WERE SHOCKED AND saddened that Sebastian and I had decided to end things, both truly disappointed. But when I explained he was moving again, they understood a long-distance relationship was not going to work at our age.

My mom held me. "I saw how you looked at him, and I saw how he looked at you. You both made a very mature decision, but I understand and sympathize with how hard it was for you guys."

I clung to her, even though Sebastian was standing with us in the form of Romy. But her sympathy was somehow so needed. Even though there was so much I wanted to tell her but felt I couldn't, I would always cherish that tender moment.

Trevor and Jimmy did a fantastic job, having my recent break-up practically old news by the time spring break was over. The first day back to school, I saw Trevor waiting at my locker. I was humbled with how emotional I became, but seeing him was the chance to tell someone about my beautiful experience with Sebastian. I wanted to tell my closest girlfriend, one I didn't have, and not being able to confide in my mom humorously left me with T.

Trevor saw my tears as I walked to him and opened his arms. I took the offered embrace with no hesitation. He whispered to the top of my head, "You okay?"

"The best days of my life."

After those words were set free, I realized that was all I desperately wanted to say out loud. His arms tightened as he rocked me. "I'm so happy for you, girl."

"She okay?" Jimmy approached behind me.

"Very." Trevor kept rocking me.

Jimmy's hand touched my back. "Oh, thank God. I thought we might've made a *huge* mistake." He leaned forward. "Who knows what kinky things *wolves* are into."

Trevor and I laughed, holding each other. Jimmy explained to nosey passersby. "See? The break-up. She's crying because of the *break-up* we told you about. Drama, whaddaya gonna do? All's well. Move along..."

Trevor whispered into my hair, "Jimmy sucks at lying."

"One of his best qualities," I answered, refusing to let him go.

During the day, I kept thinking of Sebastian and how unfair it was of me to ask him to hide again. Most girls would and should be thinking about college and what they aspired to be in life. My life was shamelessly and hopelessly wrapped around the being that I would never be able to disentangle from—never would I want to.

That night, I shared my thoughts.

Sebastian said, "Marley, if you wish for me to stop breathing, then ask me to go and live my life searching for other wolves. But if you wish for me to be happy, unbelievably content, then ask me to stay and live my life with you."

There was nothing else to say. Those words solidified that Sebastian and I *truly* were together for life because I felt the exact same way. Without Sebastian, I would cease to breathe.

So with stolen moments and whispers in the night, Sebastian and I made it to my senior year. The hallways were extremely lonely without T and Hound causing havoc and heartaches, but I was happy for them to have graduated. Instead of going to college, they got jobs. They said college wasn't for them.

Sebastian said they couldn't leave me behind until I could move on. "It's a pack thing." I hoped that wasn't true because I didn't want to be to blame for them falling behind in life.

Sebastian became an expert at transforming between Sebastian and Romy and had matured into a man over the past year. It was like an unseen force was growing inside him and developing him into the most responsible being on earth. His tendencies to watch over the house and those he considered his family were impressive. He began to stay awake and guard my parents and me at night instead of lying in bed with me. I asked if something was wrong, but he said no—he just felt taking care of us was what he was supposed to be doing.

One night, I woke to an empty bed again and quietly headed downstairs. I stopped when I saw that my mom had fallen asleep on the couch watching TV. Romy was pulling a blanket over her with his teeth.

We had tracks all over the yard where Romy would drag home big game. My dad would carve up a deer to store in our deep freezer, asking me, "Why didn't we think of this before? Saving lots of money—and your mom makes the best deer chili in the world."

Romy would sit proudly, watching us enjoy his job well done.

Another change took place in Sebastian: his need for reproduction. Not sex—he knew the difference now—but *reproduction*. Being eighteen and still in high school, I didn't think it was good timing at all. So, one late afternoon, when we were having one of our rare encounters in the woods, I pulled out a condom. Sebastian's eyes glassed over, and he *growled* at me while viewing the product that was denying his seed.

"Sebastian, you are testing me with your new behavior."

He lay next to me. "I don't know what's wrong with me."

Having put lots of thoughts into this new behavior of his, I told him, "I think this is a Romy thing, not a Sebastian thing. You don't act as young and free anymore. You seem... adultish."

Sebastian smirked. "Adultish?"

"Yes, unbelievably responsible. Making sure I'm rested and fed properly. You're practically tutoring me through the twelfth grade, and now sex has more of a purpose to you than it being an exciting activity."

"Am I not fun anymore?" He sounded disappointed in himself.

I pulled on my jeans and sat up. "I didn't say that. What I'm trying to explain is... you became a young man at eleven. And now you're maturing at that same fast rate. Your rate is *much* faster than mine. You seem ready for things I can only imagine having in the future. It's okay, Sebastian. I want to reproduce with you, but not for some years. Do you mind being patient and letting me catch up? Wait for me?"

"I think you're right. My urge for more versions of me around, as odd as that sounds, feels deeply embedded somewhere inside me."

"Of course. Reproduction is part of survival of the wild."

Sebastian thought for a moment then kissed me. "Of course I can wait. Forever, Marley."

I was done with talking mature talk and wanted playtime. "Good. Now can we have some fun?"

Wanting to please me, he said, "Yes. What would you like to do?"

I crushed my lips to his to show him what I wanted. His moan was his reply, and it gave me that shiver I loved. Sebastian must have sensed it because his kiss became primal.

Feeling awfully flirtatious, I pushed Sebastian away and jumped to my feet. With a devilish smile, I said, "If you can catch me, I promise it will be worth your while."

I ran.

My happiness was complete as I traveled deep into the woods with a wolf nipping at my heel and cool, fresh air blowing across my face. The sun was setting, and the growing darkness was exciting, heightening the freedom we were experiencing because I knew there was not an animal that could harm me with Romy by my side.

The problem was, animals weren't the only ones roaming the woods.

I laughed and screamed as Romy nipped me just right, making me tumble to the ground. My wolf became a man, kissed me in mid-roll, and by the time I stopped, he was standing as Romy again, looking mischievous and ready for more chase. I squealed and rushed to my feet, never wanting this game to end.

Romy had almost tripped me again when the bullet rang through the air.

A force catapulted my wolf into me, and we crashed to the ground. My mind never had a chance to comprehend what had happened, and I never even got to get off my back before Sebastian was dragging me into the bushes. His hands sifted through the leaves to cover the trail our bodies left behind us.

Sebastian rushed back to shield my body protectively with his, his dirty hand roughly over my mouth. I lay still, staring up at him in shock, my nose breathing heavily across the top of his hand. I couldn't help thinking of Trevor saying, "…he should not show his human form outside this house." I wanted to punch myself for not following his excellent advice.

My spine pressed into the leaves under me. I felt warm liquid begin to seep down, soaking my side. I slowly reached to touch it. When I pulled my fingers back into view, I saw blood. It wasn't mine. My wolf had been shot.

He mouthed, *"Not a word"*. I nodded but wanted him in a hospital in the next two seconds. I stopped breathing completely when I heard cautious footsteps in the leaves.

A man's voice whispered with agitation, "He was here!"

Two men were hunched over, sneaking past us with big guns in their hands, ready to fire. These were no local hunters. They looked uniformed, almost military-like, dressed in black, long-sleeved shirts, black cargo pants, and black vests with many pockets. Belts with gun holsters attached a lot of ammunition to their bodies.

My body was trying to shake in fear, but Sebastian on top of me held me still.

"I bet he rolled down that bank with the girl," the other man replied, also whispering.

More leaves crunched as the men made their way down the deep embankment, away from us.

Sebastian whispered, "They smelled of other wolves. I was not their first."

The shadow of night had set a romantic mood for our run, but now it smothered me, and I had never wanted to see the sun so dearly. I wanted the brightness to scare away the darkness that announced a horrifying scene to come.

When Sebastian felt it was time to try, we quietly crawled—well, I was practically dragged by a once again authoritarian Sebastian—out of the bushes. When we stood, I nervously began searching his body in the darkening forest, but it quickly seemed my nerves were nothing compared to his.

Sebastian strongly grabbed my hand and whispered with urgency, "No time for me. They saw you. We need to get you home. Then I'll find out what's going on."

He was the one shot, but he worried about *my* safety. Mature Sebastian had returned, and it was time to obey. His domineering energy insisted on it. So I skittishly nodded, just wanting him home so he'd let me inspect his wound. I would inform him then that he was not hunting the hunters then hope that the hunters stayed away.

Sebastian hobbled a foot ahead of me for what felt like a quarter of a mile while I did what he'd told me to do. I picked up leaves and walked backward, covering our trail and his blood in case the two men turned back, retracing their steps.

When my butt ran into Sebastian, I turned but could barely see him because it was almost pitch black. Grinding his teeth as if in pain, he struggled to put on one of the pairs of pants he kept hidden on the trails. I helped him with the button, whispering, "Are you okay?"

His eyes were glazing over. "Yes, just feel like having you closer." He put his arm around my shoulders. This was out of character for the Sebastian I had been living with for the past year. My eyes begged him for the truth as I put my arm around his waist. He smiled. "I'm fine." But he leaned on me for support. That was when I knew his injury was more than a flesh wound.

"Can't you heal yourself again?"

"Not without slipping out of consciousness, and I'm taking us the long way home in case they follow. I'm aching to get you out of harm's way. Don't worry; the bullet only grazed me."

Arguing was just going to take time we didn't have. I knew I wouldn't win with this alpha. There was no way in hell he would allow himself a nap while I forged the dark woods, with possible shooters on my trail. So I begged myself not to panic and to focus on what Sebastian wanted—*home.* "Okay, Sebastian."

The closer we got to home, the weaker he became. He was slowing down. The faint moonlight glistened off his bare chest wet with sweat. Blood, both dried and new, covered my hands. There was no more trying to fool me. "Oh, Sebastian, you're so pale." I looked down. His stomach and jeans were soaked with blood. Tears began to rim my eyes as he became heavier and heavier. He sounded so tired. "I'm sorry... I promised to never lie... to you."

Sebastian knew he could no longer hide the severity of his wound. I panted as I struggled with bearing his weight. "Lying with good intent is just another thing to love about you."

He tried to smile again but barely could while he quietly baited me. "Are you only saying this because I'm bleeding everywhere?"

I kept pulling him along as he struggled to keep his eyes open. Needing to hear his voice, I kept up the conversation. "See? You're still trying to keep me from being scared. Makes you the best, Sebastian."

His head rolled to my shoulder.

The conversation was over.

I became desperate. "Please, let's hide in a bush or something while you heal. I'll stay with you."

Sebastian slurred through his words. "Can't. They could find another... my trails... find your... parents... with no... protection."

"You have got to be the best being on this earth. Hold on. I'm getting you home, Sebastian. Please hold on."

Love, simply put, is *powerful*.

My love for him gave me the strength to carry most of his weight.

His love for me gave him the strength to hold on.

By the time we reached our back yard, I was practically dragging my best friend, screaming in hysterics, "Dad! Help me! Mom! Please!"

Sebastian feebly attempted to quiet my panic. "Shh... must... silent."

Our back door swung open.

"Jesus! Marlena! What happened?" Dad yelled as he ran down the steps, crossing the yard in an incredible rush to help his daughter, just like I knew he would.

My wonderful mother was in tow. "Why are you with Sebastian?"

I screamed. "He's been shot! Help me!"

"Shh..." Sebastian whispered, reaching out to my father as his body began to go limp *completely*. My father, the man I idolized, without knowing it, caught the love of my life in his arms. Sebastian, on the verge of unconsciousness, faintly spoke words that brought terror to me. "Everett. Danger. They're coming." Then his eyes closed.

Sebastian's phenomenal hearing must've heard the shooters approaching.

My dad looked at the young man in his arms and quietly but nervously, asked, "Who's coming?"

I rushed slightly audible words. "We may be in trouble."

"Why?" Dad asked, adrenaline almost visibly rushing through his veins, giving him strength to carry heavy Sebastian.

At that moment, when my two worlds were once again crashing together, a twig cracked in the distance. My mother's and father's bodies immediately followed the sound, as did mine. My mother and I were glued to my father's sides. With the three of us shoulder to shoulder, we began to take slow and cautious backward steps, across my yard, toward the back porch. With a bleeding man in my father's arms and having lived in the mountains all their lives, my parents instinctively knew this could be more than an accidental shooting.

Without looking at me, my father whispered, "Where's Romy?"

Until this point, I had hoped that Romy was shot by a hunter for sport or protection of their livestock, but when every little hair on the back of my neck rose, I knew the wolf hunters were much more. Locals would not be approaching my property in stealth mode if they suspected they'd injured a human by accident. And my father's friends, who were hunters, would have called out to him by now. My parents both knew this, too.

Without time to tell my parents of the potential danger they were in, I answered my father's question about Romy's whereabouts. "You're holding him."

Our shoulder-to-shoulder, slow, backward walk stopped as my parents digested my crazy words. Then it began again.

"Everett, can this be?" Mom whispered.

My father never took his eyes from the rim of his property but said, in a stern tone, "Little girl, this is *not* the time to play with me. We are being watched, and I could use that wolf's help."

When we reached the bottom step of our back porch, we stopped, wondering if we dared turn our backs and run up the stairs to get inside. My heart pounded with fear, and my voice shook. "I've been keeping a *huge* secret from you both. But... I don't think it's a secret anymore."

Another twig cracked, this time from another location in the woods.

"Everett," Mom whispered.

"I heard it."

Besides the night when I was six when my father believed he'd lost me, I had never seen him scared before until that night, the night that would change everything.

With my mom and I still glued to him, Dad began a slow backward trudge up the stairs. "In Jesus's name, I pray for strength and courage. Amelia, get my gun ready."

I began to silently sob. "I'm so sorry, Daddy."

My mom rushed into the house.

"Get behind me, baby." He still wouldn't take his eyes off his backyard, nor let go of my unforgivable lie, unconscious in his arms.

As soon as we crossed our backdoor barrier, my mother shut it quickly, aiming the gun at the door and windows. Still wearing her apron, she held the rifle masterfully. My father had trained her well. She would shoot with no question.

Through tears, I asked, "Is he still alive?"

"Yes." Dad laid Sebastian on the couch. Then he shocked the hell out of me when he grabbed my shoulders, hard. "Answer everything as fast as you can. Is this man your wolf?"

"Yes. Sebastian." I was going to answer anything he asked, and quickly.

"Two names?"

"Wolf, Romy. Man, Sebastian."

"But the same... p-person... wolf?"

"Yes. Two forms. Two names."

"Mother of God. Who are the ones outside?"

"Two men with guns. One shot Romy."

"Do they know what he is?"

"Don't know, but Sebastian had me cover our trail. Said the men smelled of other wolves."

Just then, Sebastian unconsciously transformed into Romy. My parents gasped at the bloody wolf lying on their couch on top of shredded jeans. I thought my mom was too stunned to move, but then her eyes caught movement, and she aimed at the window past our kitchen and let a bullet roar to life. As she re-cocked her gun, preparing to shoot again, the back door busted open.

My father shoved me behind him so hard I almost landed on top of Romy. My mother shot the first man to enter. His body flew back, ripping the phone from the wall before crashing to the ground.

Hell broke loose all around me.

The two men Sebastian and I had seen in the woods were now accompanied by at least four more. I couldn't be sure. That was all my mind could comprehend. With adrenaline pumping violently through my veins, everything seemed to be happening at supersonic speed. My father screamed for me to run as he charged forward. But our house was too small with too many big men. I was forced to step back onto the couch, standing over Romy, and watch madness destroy my life.

Loud gunshots went off between my mom and the gunmen before they tried to wrestle the weapon free of her small hands. Dad, fighting like a madman to get to her, stopped when he saw men trying to grab and control my kicking legs. One man had come at me from the side, managing to get his arm around my waist, pulling me from the couch. As the man turned us toward the back door, my father's powerful fist met an unsuspecting jaw. A crack of bone took place, and I was dropped from his unwanted embrace. My unsteady feet took hold just in time to see my mother fall to the old wooden floor I'd played on all my life.

She was motionless.

From that moment on, every movement that took place around me became foggy, disrupted, not whole. My legs moved of their own accord to bring me to her side. A couple of men attempted to get hold of me but were distracted by my father brutally fighting their efforts. I barely recognized my bloodied hands as I reached for my mother, rolling her to her back, my fingers shaking after touching her chest where the bullet had hit her.

The woman who had been the heart and true strength of this warm home was now lying on my living room floor with blood seeping from her body. With such a sight as your mother dying before you, something shifts inside your soul, and you just know you'll never be the same.

I wanted that shift taking place deep inside me to stop happening and tried to trick myself into believing I could change it with my very own hands. At least, that was the way it seemed as I touched her over and over, hoping I had somehow become mystical and possessed the power of healing. Desperately, I kept searching for the rewind button I needed to change this horrid outcome. If I could go back *one* moment, I could have changed destiny, possibly been fortunate enough to take the bullet myself.

My father screamed behind me as he tried to get free of the gunmen ganging up on him, fighting him. His screams told me he knew exactly what was happening and wanted to touch the love of *his* life one more time before she said goodbye forever.

Her eyes stared at me, and somehow through all of the ruckus, I could hear her last words. "Now I know… I wasn't crazy… for loving him… like a son." Her hand reached up to touch my face, but it never made it. It limply fell to the floor.

I stared at the lifeless body as all other noises around me faded, no longer intruding on my shocked senses. A tidal wave of emotions was drowning me as I realized I had not appreciated my mother as I should have. I'd never told her thank you for all the wonderful, caring things she did for me on a daily basis. Every hot bath and meal seemed so insignificant until I knew I would never feel her affections again. Now, all the love she gave me unconditionally seemed monumental. And always will.

Sebastian had told me I was strong, yet soft, and I had wondered why. What lay in front of me was why. My mother had taught me endurance and empathy with her every action. Her everyday examples were the best to learn by.

My decision to hide the secret of Sebastian had irrevocably changed my world. What I had watched Romy go through so many years ago was now happening to me. I wanted to nuzzle her for one more caress of her soft, loving hands, just as Romy had.

I began to whimper, just as Romy had.

I felt like I, too, was a howling wolf as I leaned my head back and screamed.

There was no time to stop screaming, to stop mourning or to register any pain as the butt of a rifle slammed into the back of my head, knocking me unconscious with a crushing blow.

CHAPTER FOURTEEN

TERROR TO MY SOUL

HOWLS. HOWLS THAT WEREN'T MY Romy's pulled me to consciousness. It sounded as if the howlers were being tortured in unison. Generators hummed in the background.

"What has them all stirred up? They used to stay quiet," said a voice I didn't recognize.

"Ever since *they* arrived yesterday, all the other damn wolves have been going mad and driving me nuts."

"And that gray one? What a handful!"

I presumed they were walking away because the voices faded. "Strongest wolf I've seen to date. He took a chunk out of Sam last night. Boss thinks the wolf wants the female we just passed."

"Has he converted?"

"Filed reports, but not confirmed by base."

As I awoke and my mind began to focus, memories of my mother painfully flooded my mind and heart. "Mom," I croaked out of a mouth that was now a desert. I begged my eyes to open so I could stop seeing her body, but all they did was flutter. One of the howlers changed his or her tune and began to bark, not viciously, but as if wanting to get his or her packmate's attention. I knew this because Romy used this bark often when wanting me to hear him. What I noticed was how close this bark sounded, and then I heard a clanking noise, reminding me of a chain-link fence.

I wondered how long I'd been unconscious when my eyes finally began to cooperate. I couldn't tell if the sun was rising or setting—all I knew is that I was outside somewhere. Once I could focus on what was in front of me, I saw a chain-link fence then about five feet of winter grass and dirt before another chain-link fence. It stood approximately seven feet tall and five feet wide, completely surrounding and covering a caged wolf that continued to bark.

I stared at the female wolf with green eyes and gorgeous red tints to her brown fur. Once she saw my eyes, she barked excessively and dug at the ground, trying to dig her way out. A part of me felt some relief at seeing a being in the form I knew so well. I finally found some strength to sit up, grabbing the back of my aching head. More wolves stopped the howling and began to bark. I looked around and saw many more cages, all full of wolves. It only took a few more seconds to realize that I was in a similar cage.

There were claw marks in the dirt of the inside of my confinement, showing I was not the first resident. Chills ran through my body as I saw remnants of fur from the wolf that tried to claw his or her way out. In the corner of the cage was a fence-covered entrance the size of a mail slot. A leftover bone hinted at a feeding hole. Every cage had the same slot, also with stripped bones.

Our cages seemed to make a half circle. I wondered if the circle continued, but I couldn't be sure. Big, dark-green tents similar to those you'd see on an army base blocked the view in front of me. Our chain-link doors faced this view of tents. Forest and mountains surrounded us, but not a section I recognized from all my hiking with Romy. There were no concrete or wood buildings to be seen.

As the barking continued, I spotted a bowl with water and dragged my body to it. It wasn't clean. Never had I been so thirsty that I would drink questionable water, but next thing I knew, I was lifting the bowl and drinking, water spilling in and out of my parched mouth.

A man wearing the same clothes as the men who'd attacked my family walked by but stopped when he noticed me. The big gun strapped to his back shifted as he turned to face me. "*Well*, look who made it. I thought you were a goner." There was no remorse in his voice.

My heart pounded as fear raced through me. The wolves on each side of me growled, taking a defensive posture toward the man in black.

He looked at them. "What *is* it with you mutts lately?" He glanced back to me. I stayed quiet, not knowing what to do. "Let's see if Boss can get you to talk." He walked into one of the tents. The growling ended.

Shaking, I looked around, trying to understand what was happening.

Soon, growls rumbled from the surrounding cages again. They growled, staring in the direction of the entrance to the tent where the man had disappeared. A bigger man headed out of the same tent, followed by the first man.

The big man said, "Your boyfriend will be happy you're alive." He showed no remorse either. "I am in charge of these quarters, and since I now own you, you can call me Boss. Has a nice ring to it, don't you agree?"

The wolves getting louder told me they did not.

Ghostly pale skin accentuated Boss's coal-colored eyes that looked into the surrounding cages with a puzzled expression. "This racket is bewildering, but it seems to have something to do with our new guest." He turned back to me. "How do you like your accommodations? Anything I can get you?"

He was not being nice or polite. He was condescending and the biggest asshole I'd ever met. I said nothing. I had no idea how much they knew about Romy, and I wasn't going to confirm that Sebastian existed.

"Ah." The leader paced in front of my new prison. "Quiet like your mate?" He stopped to see my reaction. I gave him nothing. "Your... *alpha*?"

Nothing. I'd done my best to keep Sebastian a secret for most of my life, and I wasn't stopping now. Boss grinned, and chills raced down my spine. He was toying with me. He knew I would not give him anything on my wolf, who was apparently tearing this place apart for me.

Boss said to his armed asshole-in-training, "Clear out this pen." He pointed to the cage holding a male wolf to my left. "I want her boyfriend to have a front-row seat." Before walking away, extremely proud of himself, he demanded, "And for God's sake, reinforce that holding!"

I swallowed, but the fear sticking to the inside of my throat remained.

From the tent, six heavily armed men approached the cage to my left. To the angry male wolf, one of them said, "No testing, so chill out. Just a relocation. You know the drill."

Two of the four men holding metal bars with wire nooses on the ends went to each side of the wolf's cage. They stuck the poles through the chain-link fencing, meeting in the middle of the cage and lining up the nooses. With one noose in front of the other, they waited. The wolf blew out a snort and walked up to the nooses, inserting his head.

Once the wolf was secure, his door swung open, and men in the front of his cage raised their guns, aiming at the wolf. The two remaining pole holders walked into the gated prison, also putting the wolf's head into their nooses. The original pole holders disconnected from the wolf, and the new holders led the wolf out of his cage with aimed guns following.

Watching him being taken away angered and frightened me. I was angry because I did not believe that a majestic animal deserved such treatment, and I was afraid because these men completed the transfer as if it were second nature to them. I was terrified how far these pros would go to get what they wanted. And not knowing what they wanted seemed to scare me the most.

The sunset had me hugging my knees because the last of any warmth was almost gone. Facing the tents, not wanting my back to the enemy, I had paid attention all day to the guards who passed me. Starting to recognize some of them, I counted approximately twenty.

I watched guards dig holes and put poles in them up against the empty cage to my left. Another guard entered the cage. He shoveled and disposed of the waste collected in a corner. Sensitive noses must have hated being next to their own feces, but obviously, they had no choice.

Soon, the sun disappeared, and floodlights attached to poles replaced its shine.

Boss had said that Romy would be delivered and put in the cage the man was cleaning, but after tragically losing my mom, I couldn't help being haunted by my reality. Anything could go wrong at any moment. The thought of losing Sebastian was too much. It almost made me vomit. Not wanting to speak and say something I shouldn't, I was not able to inquire about my father. I could only pray that he had somehow escaped and was safe. I hoped he was possibly able to take care of my mother. The thought of the shooters not treating her body with the respect that phenomenal woman deserved made me tremble.

Commotion with the wolves pulled me from my thoughts. The poop shoveler was gone, and something was transpiring on the other side of the tents to my left where I couldn't see. The wolves became extremely aggressive, growling as each wolf saw what was coming around the bend of tents. His or her posture would change to attack mode, accompanied by snarling and snapping teeth. I was so scared to see what had them this upset that I backed away from the front of my cage, crab-crawling to the rear corner.

At first, all I saw was the backs of four guards coming around the bend, aiming guns at someone or something that made them nervous, a reaction I had yet to see from the cocky pros. The men's backs blocked my view of what six more guards were doing, but every confinement they passed had a wolf viciously attacking the front of their cage.

Then I saw a sight that brought terror to my *soul.*

Romy was unconscious, being dragged by two loops or nooses around his hind legs, two nooses around his front legs, and two around his neck. Romy's tongue hung out the side of his mouth, possibly from the ropes tightening due to pressure, and his beautiful gray fur was matted in blood. His injuries looked worse than the bullet wound. Two more gun-toting men followed, ready to shoot if Romy stirred. Six guards had removed the wolf next to me. *Twelve* delivered Romy.

I got up and ran to the front corner of my cage and screamed, "What did you do to him?" I rattled my fencing with my enraged hands, not caring that I was breaking my silence.

Romy looked awful; he looked… dead. *This was what they'd reinforced the cage for?*

"Is he alive?" I shrieked in horror.

No one would take their eyes from their captive to answer me. Men opened the chain-link door to the empty cage next to mine and crudely dragged Romy inside. The other wolves gave voice to their feelings. Gunmen circled the cage as if the half-dead wolf before them had another fight in him. I'd never seen Romy more than irritated, but with how these men were behaving, I wasn't sure I ever wanted to.

Nooses were released, men ran out, and the gate slammed shut, locks nervously secured. That was when I noticed how each man had bandages somewhere on his body. Romy must had done a real number on them all.

"He's alive," one guard practically spat at me, he was so angry, "but maybe this time, he'll think twice before attacking us."

A guard high-fived him. "Showed him."

Another guard, looking braver now that Romy was locked up, sneered. "Damn *Lycan.*" His voice rose to be heard over the howling wolves. "Needed to learn his damn place."

Lycan? I thought back to the research Romy and I did on my computer. The hunters from the woods had known exactly what they were hunting and capturing.

A guard turned to the other wolves, yelling with frustration, "Shut up!"

As he and the other horrid men retreated into the tent in front of me, most of the outside lights were turned off, leaving us in the dark. Only the moon gave us light. I dropped to my knees, stretching my arm through my chain-link fencing to my bloody wolf. I didn't want to give any details away, but these men knew I was with him, so I took a chance and called out to him as quietly as possible. "Romy?"

Instantly, it went quiet. Every wolf I could see now stood in silence, watching me. For a moment, I held still, arm extended, turning to look at all the wolf eyes on me—on Romy and me. But the need to feel *my* wolf overpowered my questions about the other wolves' behavior, and once again, I reached for Romy.

It was pointless. The aisle in between us meant his cage was two inches from the tips of my fingers. I grunted as I forced my arm to accomplish something it couldn't. Unraveling, I cried out, "Romy, I'm here. Please, wake up." I didn't care anymore if someone heard me use his name.

Romy didn't move.

"I need to know you're alive, Romy." Tears choked me before I even realized I was crying. The female wolf whimpered in her cage behind me. I begged, "Please, Sebastian."

Wolves paced their cages with their tails tucked and shoulders tensed, but when Romy's paw twitched, we all froze, intently watching for more. When Romy did nothing, I whispered, "I'm here," with my battered arm stretching again. Heart-wrenching desperation came out in every word I spoke. "I need to know you're going to make it! Please, Sebastian, just one sign you're going to live through the night...Pleasssssseeeee—"

His eyes opened. They were exhausted but open.

My body collapsed into the fencing in utter relief. My exasperated lungs were finally getting the oxygen fear had denied them. "Thank you, oh, thank you, Sebastian. You can rest now. Heal, heal."

Romy's eyes closed.

I whispered, "I love you."

The wolves, softly and mournfully, howled into the night.

My mother's body fell to the ground.
Blood... her last words...
My bloodcurdling scream...

My cage door opening pulled me from the nightmare. "Mom?" I weakly called for her. But as men with weapons entered my outdoor prison, I was startled awake, realizing where I was. My eyes squinted to adjust to the sunlight. I'd made it through the night.

All the wolves were already pacing, including Romy. I sat up in a hurry, shocked to see him healed, moving easily and growling. I'd only seen him heal from the effect of four beers before. I'd been unsure of the extent of his healing capabilities. I wanted to get closer to him but had no time. I had to focus to see what kind of trouble I was in.

Three men with guns surrounded me, and then Boss entered, holding some sort of high-tech cattle prod. He grinned at Romy. "Already angry? Haven't touched her... *yet.*"

Romy barked savagely as I stayed on the ground, holding my knees to my body, watching him. Boss spoke calmly to Romy over the growling and barking of the other wolves. "Oh, yes. I think I have your attention now."

Romy viciously attacked the cage surrounding him. It rocked as his body slammed into the link walls, trying to break through. I now understood the reinforcing of his cage and why it had taken so many guards and guns to contain him. I was wrong to think Romy's rage would scare me. In fact, Romy looked beautiful. My wolf, furious in his attempt to protect me, made me proud. I looked at him in wonder and fell in love with him even more.

Boss acted as though Romy was simply throwing a temper tantrum. The man casually swung his cattle stick through the air as Romy caused havoc to his prison. It gave me an uneasy understanding of how deranged this man, Boss, truly was. My eyes followed the dancing stick while I waited for whatever was coming.

Boss finally spoke to Romy. "My field hunters claim to have seen you in human form, but, *tsk, tsk,* you refuse to convert and show me your human side. No matter what we do to you. I have to say"—he pointed to the now deformed cage—"your size and strength are alarming and impressive, but every wolf... has a weakness."

Romy froze. The cage still creaked, but Romy did not move another muscle. What Boss was up to was starting to make sense to both of us. In less than a blink of an eye, Boss was at me, and he shocked me. Painful volts jolted my body. I screamed and crawled backward to get away while Romy went berserk. The surrounding wolves joined in.

Over all the chaos, Boss yelled one word to Romy. "Convert."

Romy stopped his tirade again, and his horrified eyes looked at me. I knew he was struggling internally with what to do. His mother had told him never to reveal himself, but I was going to be tortured, possibly until he did what they demanded.

I tried to mouth, "it's okay," but Boss preferred that Romy and I not communicate. At least, that was what I interpreted the next bolt of lightning jostling my organs to be about. This time, I didn't scream. I held in my waves of nausea to make this easier on Romy.

"Reveal yourself to me, wolf, or you shall learn I'm a patient man with much endurance. How about your little mutt here? Wanna wager on how long she can take this?" He examined his fancy stick from hell. "Hmm, oh, here's the button to increase the voltage. Let's see. Had it at number three. I say we try number six. Don't worry; it goes to twelve. But I'm hoping to reason with you before *that* drastic measure."

Boss leaned over to me, preparing for his next attack. I quickly turned my back to Romy, so he didn't have to witness pain on my face. Then I closed my eyes, becoming as brave as I could, waiting for my next electrocution.

Boss's chuckle was unnerving, and his words confused me. "And *that's* how it's done, gentlemen."

Without moving from my huddled position, I opened an eye. No stick was in my view. I opened my other eye and saw the guards staring behind me. My shoulders sagged. I let out the breath I had been holding then slowly and sadly turned toward Romy's cage.

Refusing to glance at me, stood a proud, naked *Sebastian*.

CHAPTER FIFTEEN

BITTERSWEET DESTRUCTION

A GUARD PUSHED BLACK PANTS THROUGH a slot in Romy's cage. Sebastian dressed but had yet to say a word or look at me. He came back to the fence, putting his hands behind his back, standing tall, staring straight ahead, and looking pissed. From where I still sat, I could practically feel Sebastian's anger radiating from his body.

Boss seemed wickedly pleased as he toyed with Sebastian. "*Ewwww*, he's ferocious as a human, too! I bet you're dying to get your hands on me."

Boss walked over to stand next to me. "You're refusing to look at her. Hmmm. What do you not want me to know? Hmm." He squatted behind me and leaned in, still eyeing Sebastian, who only stared over our heads. "So then, you don't mind if I become acquainted with this attractive young lady?"

Sebastian's jaw clicked.

"Care to admit this is your female? Yes? If she's not yours, maybe I should let my boys have a crack at her. It gets lonely out here."

His guards all chuckled as they repositioned themselves, crudely implying what *crack* meant. I tightened my legs to my body. Sebastian did not break his empty stare, but his body began to shake. It was torture to watch *him* being tortured. Now I understood why he'd revealed himself for me. I wanted to beg Boss to stop, but I was trying to follow Sebastian's lead—say nothing.

My stomach soured as Boss took his finger and seductively ran it over my shoulders. I refused to show any weakness by withdrawing from his touch. A deep rumble escaped Sebastian's chest. Boss snickered. "I'll take that as a yes. She's yours." He stood then walked back toward Sebastian. "What shall I call you, Lycan?"

Still staring at nothing, my protector coldly answered, "Sebastian."

The wolves howled in unison. Then stopped.

Boss looked around in thought. "Their reaction to your presence intrigues me. Interested in sharing?"

Sebastian didn't budge.

"Didn't think so. How about another game? Let's play Make Your Female Convert."

Sebastian suddenly broke his stare with a blink of surprise toward Boss. "That game is impossible. She's human."

I screamed when more bolts zipped through me because Boss had indeed turned up the heat. Sebastian gripped the fencing and shook his cage. "I have done what you've asked! You are torturing a HUMAN!"

As I panted in a dazed state, Boss said, "Liar." He shocked me again.

When I could finally slow my gasping for air and see again, I realized every wolf, including Sebastian, had become a Tasmanian devil. I looked around as every prison shook, showing Boss had misjudged the wolves that had been somewhat docile until then. The confinements weren't sturdy enough for Boss to keep prodding me without a consequence. Alarms sounded, and more guards ran toward us with guns raised, fingers on triggers.

Boss pulled out a handgun, cocked it, and put it to my head. "She'll be shot before this *war* even begins. You may escape, but your mutt will be dead."

Sebastian stilled with his nose to the fencing, breathing heavily, staring at Boss. The wolves followed suit. For some unknown reason, the surrounding wolves had made it clear that they would have Sebastian's back. They stared down Boss, a silent dare to electrocute me one more time. I might be killed, but the stakes in Boss's game had just been raised.

Boss finally broke eye contact, holstered his gun, and smiled, as if he had never been challenged. "If you're willing to show me your conversion, why be secretive with hers?"

Sebastian's tight jaw refused to relax. "I don't know who you are or what you want, but She's. Not. A. Wolf!"

Boss shrugged then looked at me. "Maybe you have a weakness, too?" He pointed to Sebastian but told me aggressively, "He doesn't get fed till you convert. Your stubbornness will cause your alpha to starve." After a hand gesture from Boss, the guards started to leave.

I finally broke my silence. "Wait! I'll do anything you ask, but I can't be something I'm not. Please, don't starve him because of me." I got up and ran to the locked gate, clinging to it, pleading as the men went into the tent, ignoring me.

"Marley, stop. I don't care what they do to me as long as you're left alone."

I followed the perimeter of my prison until I was as close as I could get to Sebastian. I shoved my arm through a link, reaching out for him. Sebastian tried too, but his hands were too big to pass through. In frustration, he shook his cage again. He stopped when he saw my reaction. My panic level was rising, bordering on hysteria, as my outreached fingers begged for his touch.

His deep voice attempted to soothe me. "Shh, Marley. I'm here." His long fingers escaped captivity, attempting to touch mine.

When the tips of our fingers brushed each other, a sigh was released from my exasperated body. My eyes closed, and I concentrated on the only touch I could have. His fingers kept rubbing mine. "See? I'm here."

I nervously nodded, my face scraping across the metal.

"That's my girl." He took a deep breath as I began breathing regularly. "You're okay."

Collecting myself, I pulled my arm back inside my prison. "Are you okay? What did they do to you?"

Sebastian didn't seem to want me to get worked up again. "It doesn't matter. Are you hurt? They hit you so hard last night."

"You saw that?" I hung onto the fencing for support.

His eyes closed. "I woke to your scream. I'm so sorry about your mom, Marley."

I thought of Romy nudging her when he'd missed her on Sebastian's first day of school. I knew Sebastian was hurting too, but remembering her in the kitchen, in her apron, her bleeding body flashed through my mind. I banged my head against my cage with my eyes tightly shut. "Don't. I can't think of her and... breathe."

"Okay. Marley. Open your eyes. Concentrate on what we *do* have, for now."

I opened my eyes to see his worried grays. I nodded. "Okay. D-Do you know what happened to my dad?"

"Yes, he's caged on the other side of these tents."

His words were bittersweet. I'd hoped my father had escaped but was relieved to know he was at least alive. "Is he hurt?"

"Not much. I was in a cage near him. He talked to me. I-I listened in wolf form."

I took a deep breath. "Who are these people? What do they want?"

"I don't know exactly. Last night, when I was awake, I was a bit too destructive and distracted to listen because they wouldn't let me see you. But I think we should keep our talking to a minimum. Do you understand why?"

I nodded. I knew we did not want to reveal anything more than we were forced to.

He added, "So far, I haven't seen any video cameras or monitors watching us out here."

"Neither have I." I held up my finger. "One more question?"

He nodded.

After checking no one was listening, I whispered, "Sebastian, a-are these wolves here like you?"

Hope and dread pumped through my heart at the same time. If they were like Sebastian, they could possibly be his family. But if they were like him, they were in serious trouble.

He looked around and then stared at the female wolf behind me. "I have a"—he rubbed his bare stomach—"pull to them."

"You haven't seen any of them… change?"

He gave me a look of disapproval for me asking another question but answered. "No, but I feel I need to prepare you. These people have a tent that looks like it has a lab inside."

I found it hard to swallow again. "I've heard them use the word testing."

A metal wagon wheeled up behind Sebastian, limiting our conversation. The man pushing the cart stopped at each cage, slipping plastic trays with food and water through the same kind of slot Sebastian's pants had been shoved through. When the man got to Sebastian's cage, he goaded, "None for you," then came to my enclosure and pushed in a tray with raw meat: a skinless hind leg of an animal I didn't recognize. I looked away and closed my eyes.

Sebastian and I sat on the ground instead of inspecting my dinner further. The sun offered the warm relief I needed before the cold night to come. Spring was showing its arrival but winter had yet to let us go completely. We looked around and noticed all the wolves staying away from the raw meat we knew tempted them. The female wolf rested her snout on top of her paws, watching us with sweet green eyes.

"Sebastian, what's happening?"

He looked at the wolves purposely going hungry. "I don't know, Marley."

As the morning passed, I made a decision. "Become Romy."

"Why?"

Pulling on the raw meat, I glanced around, making sure I wasn't heard. "I'm going to feed you. If you eat, maybe they'll eat." With bloody fingers, I gestured to the wolves watching us.

Sebastian's body tensed, and his whispers were frantic. "No! Don't do anything to cause yourself harm."

"Then you'd better hurry up so I don't get caught."

Sebastian sounded unbelievably desperate, clinging to the cage between us. "Do you know what it does to me to see you hurt?" I stopped picking at the raw meat. His eyes were absolutely tortured. "After I woke and saw that man hit you, I lost it and hurt them. Then they—"

I closed my eyes, thinking about how Sebastian was brought to this cage, brutally damaged and unconscious.

"Look at me," Sebastian demanded.

I did, feeling broken.

"Don't do *anything* to give them reason. Think how many wolves will get shot if they break free to try to help us."

I felt helpless as I angrily pushed the tray away. "Okay. I just don't want you and the others to starve." I wiped my bloody fingers in the dirt and grass I sat on.

Sebastian pointed to my tray. "I'm more worried about you starving."

"Think they'll give me a hibachi grill, coal and a lighter?"

"Not likely." Sebastian checked our surroundings again.

I had tried to joke, but both Sebastian and I knew that without cooking the meat, I was possibly inviting certain kinds of bacteria into my body that might not end in my favor.

Three more days went by like that one. Demands. Threats. No food for Romy. No food I could risk digesting. And not one wolf touching what food was offered to them. I would dig a hole and take restroom breaks in the middle of the night when I hoped no one was watching and made do with grass and leaves. After my body was depleted of food, I only had to pee, and that was nowhere near as embarrassing in front of the wolves. Both Romy and Sebastian had seen that activity many times in the woods. With it being so cold, I was not as stinky as I should've been after not showering in so many days. I didn't have the energy to care, but my hair was much in need of attention.

Sebastian had begged for me to be fed, but I was not. Sebastian told me a wolf could go for lengthy amounts of time without a meal. Being a human and used to eating every day, I became so hungry I considered eating the raw meat, but after Romy sniffed it, Sebastian said, "I'm sorry. It is too far gone for human consumption. You'll become ill, Marley."

Wolves were taken away. Cages were cleaned. Sometimes, the wolves didn't return, and if they did, they were bloody and wounded. Tongues licked small areas of their exposed flesh where it appeared to have been dissected and not bandaged. It was like the ones in black were testing the wolves' healing process and immune systems or something.

The fourth night became much colder while I slept. Having no food for energy was not helping my endurance. In the middle of the night, I woke from another nightmare about my mother to a terrible fuss. The wolves were so loud I could barely hear Sebastian screaming, "She will die!" He had climbed the wall of his cage like a gorilla and was rocking his whole prison. "She is freezing and starving to death!"

Finally, four guards and Boss exited their tent. Boss said, "Lycan, your pen is starting to look crippled. Bad dog. Now what's this all about?"

Sebastian pointed to me on the ground. "Please, look at her. She's not responding to me."

I shook terribly but otherwise could not move from the fetal position. Boss nodded to his men. They entered with weapons pointed at me, as if a human Popsicle was somehow deadly.

The wolves quieted, and Sebastian pleaded, "It's got to be fifteen degrees tonight. She can't withstand this kind of exposure, especially since you refuse to blanket or feed her."

Boss countered, "No, I refuse to feed *you*, fleabag. *She* refuses to eat."

Sebastian rattled another cage wall. "You're feeding her old, raw meat!"

As he looked me over, one guard said, "Boss, her lips are blue. Willing or not, she should've shifted into a healing defense mode, being this cold."

Boss sounded somewhat human when he asked Sebastian, "Why didn't you change her?"

"She's not a fucking wolf, you madman!" Sebastian was completely hostile.

"Settle down. I'm just asking why you haven't contaminated her, Lycan?"

My mind was practically frozen, but I was still shocked at what I was hearing.

Sebastian, out of breath, looked dumbfounded. "Th-That's a myth."

Boss looked around the campsite and smiled. "Is that so?" He turned to one of his men. "Do we have a portable cage for the possible human inside the tent?"

"Negative, sir. Nothing that will withstand a change if he's lying, and unit six is full."

Boss looked to Sebastian. "Sorry, Lycan, say your goodbyes before her ears freeze and she can no longer hear you." He started walking back to the tent. Sebastian and the wolves resumed their tirades. Boss turned around and pointed to a cage with a smaller male wolf in it. "Kill that one."

A gunman walked over and aimed as the wolf backed away to try to protect himself. Wolves howled while Sebastian screamed, "NO!"

The bullet rang through the dark, cold night.

The innocent wolf never moved again.

Boss baited Sebastian. "Anything else?"

Sebastian looked defeated, as if he had failed the wolves that had been sacrificing their meals for him. "You didn't have to do that."

"Think of it as communicating. Always important to communicate."

With determination, Sebastian pointed to me. "Let me have her, then."

The guards started to chuckle. So did Boss. "Uh, let me think. No. Anything else?"

"But her heartbeat is changing again!"

Boss just stared at him with no visible emotion.

Knowing I would die and that he would have to watch or that his misbehavior would cause more wolves to die, Sebastian did the only thing he believed would gain him bargaining power. I heard the strain in his voice when he asked, "What if I change her?"

CHAPTER SIXTEEN
THE WALK OF LESSONS

IT WORKED. BOSS STEPPED FORWARD. "You would *willingly* contaminate her?" That seemed to be a key factor that piqued Boss's interest.

After a ragged breath, Sebastian answered, "Yes."

"How do I know you haven't already?"

Sebastian tried to control his frustration. "If I'm willing to starve and die for her, why would I have her freeze to death? Think! What's the point?"

"She does look pretty bad," Boss remarked with no shame for causing my miserable condition.

Sebastian growled, "Can we move this along then? I am losing her."

"What's this game piece going to cost me?" Boss inquired.

"She is to stay with me at all times," Sebastian answered, trying to get to me as fast as possible.

Boss rolled his eyes. "Too much."

Sebastian rushed out his words. "At night then. Let me have her every night so that I can keep her warm."

Boss was not hurried when he asked, "How do you know I'll keep my word?"

"What choice do I have?" Sebastian was clearly at the end of his rope.

Boss grinned. "True... okay. You contaminate her *only* when I say."

I knew he didn't want to, but Sebastian forced himself to say, "Deal." Then he whispered, "I'm sorry, Marley."

I trust you.

"We don't have to shake on it. I'd prefer to keep my hand," Boss stated.

"I respect that wise decision," Sebastian retorted. "Now, please hurry."

Boss pointed to the ground. "Sit, so they can tie you up. Any funny business, and she's dead."

Sebastian hurriedly sat on the ground and put his hands to the fencing, allowing himself to be handcuffed to the front of his cage while he watched other men try to coax me to move with the butts of their guns.

I couldn't. My hearing was fading, and my limbs refused to cooperate since they were frozen in place.

One guard asked, "Sir, you want me to carry her?"

Boss looked at Sebastian and talked through gritted teeth. "If you've lied and she attacks, we kill your mate. Understood? I don't care if the wolves go into revenge mode or not!"

"Yes, yes. Understood."

With other guns aimed and with much reservation, a young man laid down his gun and began to pick me up. I couldn't help it. I had witnessed these mean men be cruel, so I wiggled with disapproval. I instantly was dropped, and everyone started yelling out demands.

"Back away!"

"Get ready to shoot!"

Sebastian bellowed over them. "Don't shoot her! Marley! You are not to move a muscle. Do you hear me? I'm right here waiting for you, but if you move they *will* kill you. You are to let them touch you and bring you to me, Marley."

"Yes," I tried to reply, but no real sound exited my frozen mouth.

Nobody moved.

I guess Sebastian's ears could hear what humans couldn't because he hastily told Boss, "She said yes."

When the young man tried again, my body obeyed Sebastian's command and didn't move. Rapidly, I was lifted and carried out of my cage. I heard Sebastian's gate rattle with a key, and then it opened. Once again, my body was harshly dropped to the ground. Sebastian's gate slammed shut behind me. The young man was too afraid to get close to Sebastian.

"Come to me, Marley. I'll warm you."

I wanted nothing more than to be in his arms, but my body simply couldn't move. Then, with his hands still trapped, I felt Sebastian hooking his legs around my frozen body, pulling me to him. "Please, God, don't let her die." His long legs circled me tightly, trying to give warmth.

With no regard for us, the men walked away and left Sebastian tied up.

The young one who'd carried me spoke quietly. "Boss, I don't think she'll survive—absolute ice cube—but his wolf heat can probably do the trick."

They stopped walking as Boss thought.

Another guard asked, "Is this a disposable case study?"

"No, she's his Achilles heel, and he is of importance. Unlock him. And get her some cooked food."

The words "Achilles heel" caused me to fear what they would do to Sebastian now that the leader knew how far they could push him or Romy by using me.

I heard the handcuffs bang against the fence then felt shockingly warm hands grasping my face. Lips caressed mine in a hurry before Sebastian laid me down. When I didn't feel Sebastian, I heard him removing his pants. His body tried to fold around mine from in front of me as he lay on his side. Gray fur greeted me and tempted my frozen fingers to latch on. I burrowed myself into his midsection. His front and back legs sheltered me, over my head, under my feet, and two legs draped over me. A wet snout sniffed me and inspected me.

One by one, my muscles began to relax, relishing in the warmth my Romy offered. Eventually, I was even able to slowly roll over to heat my back against his soft chest. I'd missed my furry best friend and this wonderfully familiar, comforting embrace.

A tray sliding through Sebastian's slot made me stir. I did not want to see one more slab of raw meat I could not eat. But when a stick pushed the tray the rest of the way in front of me, I could barely believe my eyes. There was a peanut butter and jelly sandwich, an apple, and a small bottle of milk.

A whisper told me, "I'm sorry I couldn't get you something warm to eat at this hour." It was the voice of the man who had carried me.

My hungry hand shook as it reached out, afraid it was being tricked. My fingers sank into the soft bread, and my eyes welled. I quickly took a bite and thanked the man making his way around the cage.

"You're welcome, ma'am." He was surprisingly young.

"How old are you?" I shakily asked.

"Eighteen."

"So young."

"So are you," he said with a hint of regret.

I thought of my mom, my dad, and my present predicament. I felt older than ever. "Not anymore, I'm afraid." I tried to reach behind me with my sandwich. "Romy, take a bite."

One bark.

"Please, Sebastian. Tell Romy to eat."

One bark.

"I was afraid he would take your food from you."

I weakly said, "Not this stubborn alpha," and took another bite. A simple PB and J had *never* tasted *so* good. The young man had sorrowful eyes as he walked away.

Burrowing into Romy while he guarded and warmed me, I felt safe for the first time in days. I knew the chances of feeling this miraculous way again were slim to none. Sebastian and I were most likely going to become lab experiments and possibly meet a gruesome end. Before my life ceased, I wanted one more moment with Sebastian. My fingers ran through the fur under his chin. *So soft.* "Romy? Please become Sebastian for me."

He whimpered.

"I know it's cold, but I'm much warmer now and…" I began to cry. "I need to kiss the man I love."

A bare-skinned chest appeared. I inhaled Sebastian and moaned in deep satisfaction as I felt his arms surround me, as if promising more safe moments. "Marley, this is not the end." His hand touched my face. "Don't give up."

I looked into his eyes. "Kiss me. Let me have this."

Sebastian surrendered to my request with urgency. He kissed me with so much emotion we both were crying by the end. Our tears mingled as he rubbed his face all over mine. "Oh, Marley. I missed touching you like this."

I kissed him again. "Thank you for giving us this moment."

I regretted that Romy had to return, but I was trembling again. Sebastian's expression told me he adored me. His words told me the same. "No matter what they do to me, know this—I will love you forever, Marley."

I choked on tears because I felt as if we were saying our last goodbye. "Sebastian, our love will stand the test of time. It will never die… even if our bodies do."

One last beautiful kiss was placed on my lips before Sebastian allowed Romy to warm me through the rest of the night.

The sun on my face told me I'd made it another night. The wolf's heavy breathing in my ear told me why. Getting to sleep next to him, as I had for most of my life, left me feeling rested and, for the first time since my mother passed, free of nightmares.

Still spooned by Romy, I heard footsteps and men talking as they came and went. Soon, I heard and felt the rumble of Romy's growl. I knew what that meant; they were here to remove me.

"You promised to behave," a man warned Romy. "Keep your end of the bargain, and she'll be back tonight."

Since he didn't even like another's scent on me, I was sure Romy would be fighting his possessive side. I was almost happy to know Romy was going to fight for me because I didn't want to lose this feeling of comfort and safety. I refused to open my eyes and accept that our wonderful evening together was crashing to an end.

I was surprised to feel Romy lick my face and then experience his heat leaving my body. When my eyes opened, Sebastian was putting on his borrowed black pants. With an expression I could not read, he knelt down and grabbed the apple I had not eaten. "Please eat this today."

I slowly nodded, accepting the apple in a confused state. I couldn't fathom why Romy was letting me go. Sebastian stood and reached his hand out for me. I took it and stood as he silently asked me to. His arms embraced me, and he whispered in my ear. "Forever, Marley."

His expression made more sense to me. Sebastian was heartbroken. He sensed how I was going to react to being separated from him. And he was right.

I clung to him and my apple as he made his way to the front of his cage, silently pleading to him to not let me go. I followed him to the ground and sat in his lap as he took his position to be handcuffed again, not letting my pleas deter him. My hands followed his as he raised them to the fencing in one last attempt to stay by his side. I jolted as I heard the key wrestling with the lock on Sebastian's gate. I unraveled in fear.

"No, no, no," I moaned.

"Shh, my Marley. Be brave." Sebastian tried to soothe me while rubbing his head on top of mine. I hid in his neck, kissing him, begging for his protection. What I didn't realize at the time was that he *was* protecting me. Sebastian was fighting every instinct Romy shot through him, wanting me to be left alone. What Romy didn't understand was that Sebastian knew they would hurt me to control him and not shed a tear over it. The wolves meant nothing except experiments and results.

"Ma'am?"

Clinging to Sebastian's bare chest, I dared to look behind me at the sound of kindness. The guard who had brought me food last night, the same young man who'd carried me into Sebastian's cage, now held out his hand, gently saying, "It's okay."

Another black-dressed man smacked him on the back of his head. "What are you doing? She's one of them."

The young man stood angrily. "She is *human,* and my oath said to protect humans!"

"Stand down," Boss said, exiting the tent. "He's right—*if* she's a human. Take her to unit six for blood testing. Maybe she won't be inconclusive like the rest."

Sebastian spoke in my ear. "You can do this, Marley. Eat that apple to help your sugar level."

The young man in black squatted and reached out his hand again. "Please, ma'am."

He was doing what he could to help me. I chose to do the same. I kissed Sebastian hungrily. He responded. Then I took the hand offered and was led away.

Behind me, I heard Sebastian say, "You know we're not lying, or you would have guns out, not just one guard escorting her."

Boss replied, "Until we know otherwise, we'll keep her injuries to a minimum."

I watched over my shoulder. Sebastian's fists were iron tight. "What do you mean? Don't hurt her! We have a deal!"

A laugh was the only reply.

Sebastian rattled his cage, screaming, "We had a deal!"

I tried to keep looking behind me, but the young man who had a hold of my arm convinced me otherwise. "Don't look. He wouldn't want you to see this."

I faced forward. Then I heard a thud. All went quiet.

My knees gave. My next step faltered. The kind guard tightened his hold, keeping me from hitting the ground. He whispered, "He told you to be brave. Breathe."

Tears fell from my eyes as I continued my journey to unit six, hating my weakness.

Through my sniffles, I heard a lapping. I looked to my left, and saw as I passed each cage, each wolf tried to lick through his prison. The young man looked behind him to see if anyone was watching. "What the…?"

Sebastian was right; no one was following us—no one was afraid of me. The young man guided me closer to the holdings. "What do they want?"

I reached out my hand. The wolf's tongue licked my fingers over and over. I sadly answered, "To give affection." My finger reached through the fencing, and I rubbed the wolf's nose, returning the endearment. "If they're anything like Sebastian, they are the kindest souls you will ever know."

The guard gestured for me to move again, mumbling, "I hate my job."

"I hate your job, too."

When we walked around the bend of tents, I saw I was correct. All the cages made a huge, circled border. On the other side of the green tents that was my view from my cage, was a white tent.

"Marlena!"

I looked for my father. I soon saw him caged, yelling again. "Marlena!"

"Dad!"

"Baby, you're alive! I thought I'd lost you, too." My father clung to the fencing.

The words "lost you too" stung me so quickly that worry for where I was headed faded, and the memories of my mother reappeared.

I eyed a bandage around his bicep. "Are you hurt?"

"No. No, little girl. Are you?"

I lied too. "No. I'm okay."

I tried to get closer to my father, but the young man stopped me. "Sorry, we're here." He gestured for me to enter a big white tent.

My father lurched to the fence. "No! Please don't take her in there!"

He must've seen what went in and *how* they came out.

The young man looked around then quietly said, "Only blood work, Everett. Please stop drawing attention to yourself."

Knowing I was about to disappear again, my father frantically asked, "Where's Romy?"

"A cage next to mine. They're letting me stay with him at night for warmth."

My father's shoulders sagged in relief. He looked at me with his heart exposed. "I'm glad you have him. He loves you." As I was taken into the tent, he yelled, "I'm not mad you didn't tell me, Marlena. She wouldn't have been mad either. His secret is sacred."

My father telling me he wasn't angry that my mother had been killed because of my lie had me on the verge of hysterics. My chest heaved as I looked over my shoulder, not wanting to lose sight of him. "I love you."

With a despairing expression, he told me, "I love *you*, little girl."

That was when the cage next to my father's caught my attention. This wolf was huge, almost as big as Romy, and black, but he looked mean, and he was staring directly at *me*. My blood went cold.

In the tent were stainless steel tables big enough to hold big wolves with shackles and restraints of all different sizes. I could practically smell death. One table had a smaller, unconscious wolf strapped down. My heart bled for him. He was hooked up to a drip full of yellow fluid and a heart monitor. Machines beeping with data and portable chalk boards reading "subject: negative reaction to acid test…" confirmed that experiments were taking place.

Other stainless steel tables had disturbing tools, including saws and large syringes, along with items I did not recognize. There were cages, some occupied by sickly wolves with pus running from their noses and ears and bald patches in their fur. One cage held a gorgeous ivory wolf, sleeping on his side.

A man with a white doctor's coat almost covering his black clothes examined his chart. He looked at another man dressed the same way. "Deceased. Need another removal."

I gasped. The bastards had killed him.

At my noise, the man with the chart glared at me. "Ah, the female controlling our troublemaker." To the young man holding my upper arm, he said, "Sit her over there."

Hopeless wolf eyes watched me through bars as I was guided to a chair.

Putting the chart in a holder with the other charts, the first man asked, "Count?"

"Forty-seven changed successfully. Seventeen of those have survived testing. Six originals still existing and one contamination to do."

The man who'd nonchalantly spoken of another wolf's passing walked to me with a different chart. "Only blood? Damn, I'm waiting to get my hands on you to see what makes ya tick and how you'll react."

My voice trembled. "React to what?"

He grabbed an alcohol swab. "Wouldn't you like to know."

True to their word, only blood was drawn. I tried to stand afterward but became extremely woozy.

My kind guard helped me sit back down. "You should eat that apple."

I nodded timidly and ate. I wanted to become invisible and find a key to release all the captives.

When I exited the tent, my father was waiting. "Are you hurt? I didn't hear you scream." His face was stricken with worry.

I didn't envy my father's front-row seat to the hell taking place in the white tent. "Just took blood. Dad, who's next to you?"

My father weighed the questionable wolf snarling with a critical squint. "Just an angry old bastard."

The wolf snapped his teeth at my father.

I was ushered away. My father clung to his fencing, his gaze following me. His eyes were trying to tell me so much. "Listen to my words carefully. Stay. With. Romy. No matter what. No matter what you see, little girl."

Pain stabbed my stomach. I sensed his words were a warning of sorts. I began to fight the young man restraining me. "Wait! Dad, what do you mean?"

"No, don't fight John." My father looked at the young man who was nervously glancing around, checking for witnesses. I nodded and stopped pulling on him. With such a heavy heart, my father told me, "Choose Romy. It's what I want."

I said nothing. I felt disloyal without knowing why.

My father yelled, "Promise me!"

My father *yelling* at me told me the severity of his words. Even though I didn't understand them, I understood what he needed to hear. Losing sight of my father as I was taken back around the bend, I told him, "Okay, Daddy. I promise."

I chose the word *Daddy,* so Dad knew I would be the obedient child he was asking for. His tender smile told me he got the message. I'll never forget that smile. *Never.*

Whimpering wolves seemed to want me. Remembering the dead wolf and the ones suffering in unit six made me reach out and try to touch each and every caged wolf I passed. In return, I received licks of encouragement, licks of strength that woke the woman in me, the fight I needed to no longer be afraid.

A need to take care of these beautiful creatures awakened the mother in me.

These wolves had growled for me, had attacked their cages for me, and were starving for Romy. One had died for me. I looked into many different shades of eyes as I took the walk that changed my perception on life and gave silent promises to do all I could to see them safe and free again.

My incredibly brave mother had died protecting me. I would show that her strength did not die with her. It was passed on to me, and I was willing to make the same sacrifice for those I considered my new family, including the alone, unconscious Sebastian who was still in the same position as when I left, limply hanging from his restraints attached to his cage. I swallowed my anger, hiding it in a special place for when I was ready to release it.

I was surprised when John stopped in front of Sebastian's cage and began unlocking his gate. I walked through the opening. As John locked me in, I quietly asked, "Can you please un-cuff him now?"

The young man looked at the keys in his palm, thinking, then back at me while going to Sebastian. His eyes were trying to talk to me the way my father's had. As before, I didn't understand, but I knew it didn't matter. A connection was forged between John and me, and when his message needed to be clearer, it would be.

Dried blood told me how a guard had hit Sebastian in the head, knocking him out. Had they untied him, Sebastian could have transformed back to Romy and healed again. I knelt next to my love and gently touched his beautiful face. Released, his body slumped over and fell to me. I sat on the ground, leaned my back to the wall of our prison, and stretched out my legs as I rested his head in my lap. I ripped off a piece of my dirty shirt, dipped it in his water, and softly wiped the dried blood from his skin. After cleansing him the best I could, I ran my fingers slowly through his thick, dark hair. There wasn't anything else I could do for him. I could only hold and watch over him until he or Romy returned to me.

Sebastian did not stir until the afternoon. He seemed to be struggling in a nightmare, calling for me. "Marley..."

I kept rubbing his hair and touching his face. "I'm here. I'm here, Sebastian."

Sebastian was lucky. He woke in a blissful mood, completing forgetting where he was and the nightmare he'd just experienced. With his face in my lap, facing my belly, he inhaled and smiled when his eyes opened. His arm strongly wrapped around my waist. "Marley, waking up with you is my most favorite way to open my eyes."

I tried to smile, waiting for him to remember. "Oh yeah? Why's that?"

His eyes closed as he nuzzled me. "Because I'm in love with you."

I'm in love with you, too.

"Marley?"

"Yes?"

His eyes opened again, and he smiled so genuinely that my heart broke. My eyes brimmed at the sight of what joy I brought him, even in such madness. His mouth opened, closed, opened. "Will you marry me?"

"What is marriage?" asked Sebastian as we sat in my living room with the shadows of the muted TV shining across our faces.

I looked at the pictures on my living room wall. Some were of when I was younger. In one picture in particular, my mother was kissing my father's cheek with such affection it melted my young heart.

"It is love, being given a promise of commitment for life. Some say even longer."

Tears fell.

I could barely speak because of the memory of the love my parents had and because the happiest moment of my life was going to be tainted once Sebastian remembered where we were. "Yes, Sebastian," I softly answered. "I will marry you."

Sebastian got a seductive look in his eyes. I knew what he wanted and so desperately wished I could offer it to him. He pushed off the ground, getting to his knees. His lips looked ready to kiss mine, but when his eyes caught sight of the cages, he froze. Recognition replaced his bliss. His eyes found mine. My eyes apologized to him for allowing him to believe he was free.

I rose to my knees and faced him.

From the happiest to the worst.

My breath was stolen as he grabbed my face and placed a deep kiss on my lips. He moaned as he ravaged and conquered more of my mouth. The fact that the only TLC my teeth had received was my finger and a dirty water bowl should have revolted him, but I guess life and death make these little things, well, not so important.

In a breathy voice, he said, "I meant every word. Don't you ever doubt me or my words to you." He kissed me again.

We were on our knees in a powerful embrace during the worst time of our lives, and I swear I touched a place in heaven that beautiful, miserable day.

CHAPTER SEVENTEEN

INHERITING ESSENCE

S EBASTIAN SAT IN THE BACK corner of our cell. I sat between his legs, leaning on his warm chest. As he played with my dirty blond hair, he asked, "What did they do to you?"

"Drew blood. Nothing else."

His head leaned affectionately against mine. "Why did I get you back before night time?"

"I don't know. Maybe Boss felt guilty for the concussion? Sebastian, have you ever seen the... mean wolf over there?"

He kissed my cheek. "Yes. Why?"

"He was in the cage next to my dad. He scared me."

His body tensed. "Did he hurt you?"

"No, but... he wanted to, I think."

"But your dad is okay?"

"Besides having a view of the devil's tent?"

He shivered. "Horrid view. Hearing it is bad enough."

I'd forgotten about his sensitive hearing. I looked around at all the sensitive ears. More anger built inside me as I realized these wolves were forced to hear their kind tortured. I wanted someone to pay for it.

I felt Sebastian look over his shoulder, so I peeked around his big bicep. A wolf I hadn't seen before was being led by poled nooses. I understood why I'd been put back in Romy's cage when the new wolf was placed in mine. Boss and his docs were running out of room.

When the wolf was left alone, his hunched body trembled, tail tucked between his hind legs. I left Sebastian's lap and crawled toward the timid wolf. "It's okay. You're not alone. My name is Marl—"

His wolf form spasmed, stopping me on my knees, and then he fell to the ground, violently turning into a human. Young green eyes opened. He seemed to be only around fourteen.

My heart instantly bled for him. "You're okay. Just try real hard not to fight it."

"Wh—Why are they doing this to me?" he asked with an extremely shaky voice. He contorted with agony on his face and then shifted right back to wolf form. He seemed to have no control over the transitions.

I froze in fear when the new wolf now lunged at his own fencing to get to me. But I didn't even have time to scream. My gray wolf stood over me, viciously growling his warning. I had never witnessed his transformation at lightning speed before. It was beyond amazing.

After looking above my shoulder at the massive, rumbling chest above me, I saw the now-cowering wolf, pitifully urinating on himself as he backed away. When he jolted and switched into a human, something seemed off about his transition. It wasn't fluid—it didn't look natural.

The teenager appeared lost and confused. "What is happening to me?"

Romy stopped growling, my back to his chest. With my fingers grasping the chain links, I said, "Try to embrace your—"

Slamming back into wolf form, the teenager launched at me again. This time, neither Romy or I reacted because it was too shocking. We both froze as this poor, tortured soul violently switched back and forth in between forms, sometimes stuck in an agonizing mixture of the two. It was as if his body couldn't properly conform to its new shape or reason. Nature and an abomination fought for control.

In sweaty human form, he reached out to us. "Help me."

My skinny hand reached through the hole, but he was too weak for us to connect—for him to touch one more caring person before he passed. No, the last touch he would know was to be from cruel creators who ultimately killed him. Slowly, I withdrew my hand and rested it over my saddened heart.

Sebastian's hands gently touched my shoulders. Still on my knees, I quietly pivoted and sat back into the lap and arms waiting to comfort me. The male wolf next to our cage sat on his hind legs. He inhaled deeply as guards approached his kennel with nooses. I heard the female wolf, imprisoned next to my old cage that now housed death, behind me pacing. Sebastian and I could only sit silently as we watched another wolf be led away to meet his fate.

A couple of hours later, the metal wagon came around, feeding wolves. The man in the bloody white clothes with the meal cart did not appear to be a guard. He pushed a tray of raw treats into our cage. My stomach turned.

"Damn it. I should have bargained for you to be fed," Sebastian complained over my shoulder. But then a tray with baked chicken, salad, bread, and a glass of milk was pushed in. I leapt from Sebastian's lap and grabbed the links restraining me, telling the wolves, "He has food. Please, don't refuse to eat any longer."

Exasperated because the wolves didn't move to eat, I looked back at Sebastian, who… smiled. I told him, "Now eat, so they will."

Sebastian became Romy, tearing into the meat on the tray. He was starving! But I froze when no other wolf touched his or her food. "Please! He's eating now!" I was beyond upset with the dead wolf in the cage next to me and the rest going hungry.

The wolves just stared at me. Romy sat next to his tray, chewing and watching.

Completely frustrated, I sat heavily next to my food. Too upset to eat, I numbly poked at my plate. From the corner of my eye, I saw some movement. The female wolf one cage over crept closer to her tray while watching me. It started making sense to me. I picked up my chicken, and she got even closer. I shoved chicken in my mouth. I spoke around the poultry, "Nah wah ya eut?"

Raw meat was suddenly being devoured with a vengeance by all the surrounding wolves. They were finally not refusing their meals. If I hadn't been so hungry myself, I was sure I could've cried again, but instead, I did some devouring of my own. Romy rubbed his body against my back before following suit, eating more of his food. Huge wolves crunching through dead animals would deter some appetites, but I grew up with Romy, and his eating habits deterred me not at all.

Two nights later, John approached our cage with a blanket and a barrel of wood for a fire because it had snowed and snowed. The sun was still setting far too early, causing long, cold evenings and nights. Romy lifted his head to observe the activity. All guards were on deck, ready to deal with a hostile wolf. I peeked out from my Romy cocoon. "If no one touches me, this wolf will not move. John, I assure you, you will be unharmed, and these men can get out of the snow."

All the guards shifted from one foot to the other, trying to stay warm. It was bloody cold, a freak snowstorm as winter's goodbye present.

Boss shivered violently. "I believe her. Good luck, John. We'll be watching your back from, uh, inside." He didn't believe me, but he left one of his own behind out of selfishness.

John's jaw dropped as the other guards followed their leader, leaving him in the freezing cold to deal with hell on paws by himself.

Shivering, I said, "It's okay. I give you my word, John."

Romy laid his head back in the snow to continue to rest and confirm my promise.

"See? He's a big ol' pussy cat."

Romy growled.

I laughed. "Big ol' dog?"

Another growl.

"How about a big bad wolf?"

Silence.

I winked at John with snow on my eyelashes. "Even wolves have egos, I suppose."

John's cold, trembling hands shook as he went through his keys. "I can't believe I'm doing this, but I'm too frozen to stop and think about what a horrible mistake this is." He unlocked the cage. "Please have pity on me, and keep him from eating me alive."

"Lucky for you, he's already had dinner."

John froze.

"I'm kidding!"

"Not funny." John smiled.

He wheeled in the barrel and started unloading. "Want me to start the fire so he can keep you warm?"

"Get your ass in here!" Boss yelled from the warm tent.

"Thanks anyway." I half shrugged under the weight of Romy's massive front leg.

John approached. "Here're the matches." He stopped when Romy lifted his head.

I tapped his snout. "Don't be a bully. John here means me no harm." I reached out for the matches.

John slowly handed them to me, but Romy refused to lie back down. "Easy, Cujo."

I gasped.

"What? Oh shit, did I offend him?"

Romy finally put his head down with a puff from his nose.

"No," I told John. "Just reminded us of a friend."

Trevor.

Boss even permitted John to occasionally bring me more dry wood throughout the evening before stocking us up for the night. John didn't have Sebastian locked up. He just entered our cage at will, trusting Romy, adding wood to the fire. John whispered, "Boss is taking Romy's obedience as a reward for letting you be in here." He raised an eyebrow with a questioning slant.

John was young but saw right through my plan. I was trying to build trust between us so if needed, I had a human comrade as backup. I smirked. "I have no idea what you're insinuating."

Romy grunted.

John smiled. "Huh. Romy seems to see what I'm implying."

"Oh, he's just a dog. What does he know?" Again, I was trying to show John Romy's playful side.

It worked. Romy growled, and John played. "Not a dog, remember?"

I smiled from the huge wolf's embrace. "I forgot. Oops!"

The fire melted the snow on the ground, causing a slushy mess, so Sebastian—not allowing me to move from my cocoon—pulled me into dry snow as needed, taking me further and further from the fire. With not as much heat, Romy and my blanket sheltered me as best they could. I lay in the fetal position, facing the fire and the female wolf, tucked in a tight ball, half covered in snow.

I closed my eyes to fall back to sleep. Romy and my back were to the other cage. I was surprised to hear the gate open and close, but not enough to face the cold and inspect. The male wolf normally occupying the space had been gone all day. I didn't want to witness another dissected, innocent wolf.

After boots crunching the snow quickly disappeared into the tent to seek warmth, Romy turned into Sebastian and whispered, "Oh, my God."

My eyes opened, and I peered out from my blanket igloo. My jaw dropped. The female wolf that had stayed silent for all these days was now standing, naked, in the snow. The fire glowed brilliantly against her red hair. Her slender body basked in the light of the moon shining down on us. Her green eyes practically glowed. I noticed an alarming scar of what looked to be teeth marks on her left thigh.

Something had triggered her to transform and finally show herself. Her eyes narrowed, and she ignored Sebastian and me gawking at her. "Are you okay?" Her voice was divine and gentle with an accent I couldn't place.

A male voice with the same accent whispered from behind us. Sebastian and I sat up to see who it was.

The wolf who had shared this hellhole campground with us was now a blond, naked man lying on his side in the snow. "I am, but they're not." He pointed to Sebastian and me. He sat up, crossing his legs in the snow to be discreet about his exposed self.

Every wolf in sight watched. I wondered if the rest were listening.

Sebastian wrapped the blanket around me and pulled me into his lap to keep me off the snow. Our backs were to the tents, so we could see both newcomers.

Sebastian whispered to the man, "What has you so spooked that you risk showing yourself?"

Softly, to keep from being heard by the enemy, the man answered. "I heard information I must share with you." He looked at the female and winked. "Stop worrying. Your male is hard to break."

Her whisper's volume rose. "I'm breaking by not being able to touch you."

I gasped. They were *together*, yet they kept it hidden. I guess they didn't want to experience what Sebastian, Romy, and I were enduring.

The blond man looked at Sebastian, waiting. Sebastian squeezed me, probably scared of what he was about to hear, and then nodded.

The naked man quietly spoke. "They plan on changing her."

Sebastian nodded. This we knew.

"But... not by you, my leader."

Sebastian's body jerked in shock. "Wait. What did you just call me?"

Many of the surrounding wolves lifted their snouts to the sky, as if wanting to howl, but they stayed silent. I understood when they looked at the tent. They didn't want to attract the humans.

From the other man in a cage, a playful eyebrow brought my attention to blue eyes with white cloud designs, just like Romy's. Having observed this male wolf for so long, I couldn't believe I hadn't noticed those eyes before now. I figured it was a werewolf trait. The blond man asked, "Which part, Sebastian, son of Mercio, our fearless leader?" He looked to the sky to honor someone who had passed. "May he live with his love in the stars."

Father Wolf.

"In the stars," the redheaded beauty whispered with her head bowed and her eyes closed.

Sebastian and I were speechless.

"Your mother was my mother's sister," the naked man stated. He smiled. Those eyes weren't a werewolf trait; they were a *family* trait.

Sebastian body jolted and twitched with every word this man spoke. "I... have... family?"

"Yes, many of us."

"W-Why... am I not with you?"

The blond man went to answer, but Sebastian interrupted. "Wait, my cousin. What is your name?"

Another smile appeared as he tilted his head in respect. "My mother loves the history of gods. I am Zeus."

I couldn't help it. An image of a wolf sitting casually in the woods, flipping pages in a history book, passed through my mind.

Sebastian's cousin's happy face faded. "Your mother and father took you from harm's way. The wolf Marley spoke of, the mean wolf, is your uncle, Maximus—your father's brother. He is the one who is to change your mate."

Behind me, Sebastian's body went rigid.

The woman gasped. "No."

Zeus said to her, "Agatha, my beautiful, become a wolf, and keep our secret safe. I do not wish to be tortured as Sebastian has been with his Marley." Her eyes closed, and she rubbed her face on the fencing as if imagining his touch. Her wolf form took shape. Zeus said, "Agatha's reaction is because she understands the danger of such a bite. The one who inherits you—"

"Inherit?" I asked.

He smiled again as his posture straightened. "Yes, to inherit one is to choose them, evolve them, contaminate someone—as Boss so crudely defines it—and when you inherit them, an essence of yourself lives within the someone special you've chosen, as I now live within Agatha."

Zeus made the process of becoming a wolf sound like such a privilege, an honor to be chosen. I saw the majestic red wolf sitting proudly, watching the one who inherited her.

Zeus said, "That is why your bloodline will always lead. Your father's bloodline, his family's essence, distantly lives in us all. We originate with the essence that you are directly made of, Sebastian." Zeus's eyebrows furrowed as he looked at the ground. "Your uncle's essence has been irreversibly tainted with his choices and is *not* what you want in the blood and soul of one you love so dearly." He pointed to my old cage, where the young boy had died.

Arms tightened around me. "And he wants to change Marley?"

"No, my leader. Boss wants him to change her. Your uncle wants to kill her."

I shook, not from cold but from chills of a whole other kind. "Why?"

Zeus spoke with what I can only describe as wisdom. "I wish I had a good reason for why your Uncle Maximus wishes you and yours harm, but I do not. It's the old story of jealousy that has happened through many events in history and now has become part of *our* history. Maximus wants to end your reign, Sebastian."

I was entranced and hung on Zeus's every syllable.

"A leader named Gabino had two sons, Mercio and Maximus. When he chose Mercio to be our next ruler, Max became envious. The envy, over years, became more. It ate away Max's purity and manifested into darkness while he waited and plotted. When his father, Gabino, your grandfather, passed to join the stars, the time had come for Max to execute his plan to kill your father without anyone suspecting him and take what he felt to be his rightful place as our leader. But Sebastian, when your mother became pregnant with you, the wolves rejoiced, and your uncle's plan went awry because your mother went under the normal protocol of protection." Zeus grinned proudly. "She was carrying such value."

"Value—a gift only a female wolf can offer through birth. And with this gift being next in line to lead, your uncle concocted a story of unknown betrayal within our wolves. Maximus, your uncle, had to remove you if he were to ever have a chance to lead us. Panic spread, and your father did what he thought best. He removed you and your mother from any possible threat and was going to guard her and his unborn until the pup was strong enough to fight whatever threat approached."

Sebastian sounded angry. "Did my uncle kill my father?"

"It would give me much joy to give you peace with an answer about your past, but I don't have one for you. What I do know is that your uncle was soon found to be guilty of false rumors, and since your grandmother couldn't find the courage to permit the execution of her son—"

"I have a grandmother?" Sebastian struggled to swallow.

"Yes, a feisty old pup. We have very long lives when the source sees it fit." Zeus became silent, allowing Sebastian a moment to catch up.

In the quiet moments, I thought about what Zeus said—*the source*. I knew in my heart that was what they called God—what Sebastian claimed to feel around him at all times.

Sebastian inhaled deeply and then nodded.

"Your grandmother is watching over your sister and leading us again. Your sister was not able to reign because she does not have the heart of an alpha. She is far too kind and easily persuaded."

My cold hand covered my gaping mouth.

"A-A s-sister," Sebastian stuttered. Then he became angry. "My uncle tried to hurt her?"

With a smile, Zeus gestured to Sebastian. "No, she is unharmed, but see how quickly you prepared to defend without even knowing her? That is the trait of a true alpha. This is why your father did not choose your sister to lead us. He was waiting for you. We understood this, as does she. She is a gracious young wolf."

After giving Sebastian another moment to digest all this information, Zeus continued. "Your uncle was set free but ordered never to return. He did not. I believe he hunted your father down, not to become our leader— that was no longer an option—but out of revenge. Your grandmother never lost hope that her mate chose Mercio, your father, to lead for a reason. And over the years, she had us, a select few, search for her son's successor. She claimed, 'He would not have failed.' We searched and searched woods all over the world. Your grandmother has relocated us many times in our search. Now, the pack resides in Canada. I'm ashamed to say I started losing hope and wanted to start a family of my own with Agatha. But everything changed a month ago, when we came across the remains of a wolf. A very *large* wolf. We knew it was Mercio, the only other wolf to match the size of *his* father. The same size as you, Sebastian.

"We rushed home to tell your grandmother of our findings, to give her peace of mind that we had found her son. Then we came back in search of your mother. We picked up a male's scent, and the trail led us to wolf bones in a shallow grave. You visited your mother often."

Sebastian rocked us back and forth. Zeus's eyes watered. "That is how we knew—how we knew *you* existed. Who else would have taken the time to bury a wolf but a child?"

I rubbed on the arms around me to give Sebastian some comfort as we rocked together.

"We were following your trail, and were so excited to have *finally* found you that we were extremely distracted and became easy captures for this place. We were brought here, and that's when I learned your uncle's fate and how his bite had made more just like him."

Sebastian growled. "He will not touch Marlena. My Marley."

Zeus looked intrigued. "*Marlena.* I suspected Marley was an endearing nickname with the way you speak it." The surrounding wolves puffed air out their mouths as if wanting to make sounds but restraining themselves. Zeus smiled at them. "They like Marlena, feel she's a good match for their leader. That is why they wouldn't eat. We watch over our own."

Their own.

Zeus faced us again. "Even though she came to this place separate from you, your scent was all over her. We understand how males get when their female is at her fertile time."

"What?" Sebastian asked.

"That is why he growled at me when I insisted on a—" I was too embarrassed to say condom, so I whispered, "Protection?"

Zeus quietly chuckled at my question. "Of course. You were asking him

154

to deny one of nature's strongest instincts. Did you see his body tremble when Boss threatened to share you?" He quietly laughed again. "Luckily for Boss, Sebastian is unaware of his true strength, or Boss would already have been removed from this world." Zeus inhaled deeply. "Sebastian, unfortunately I do not have spare moments to help you tap into your powers. That takes time, so there is only one way to stop your uncle from inheriting Marlena."

Sebastian was not asking questions I would have expected. *"How powerful will I be?" "What powers will I have?"* No, he was only worried for me. "Tell me. I will do anything for her." Sebastian kissed my hair over and over. "Tell me what to do, Zeus."

Zeus spoke proudly. "Inherit her yourself. Tonight."

Until that moment, I think Sebastian and I believed we would find a miracle and get out of here, unscathed, unchanged. But as it all sank in, I knew I had already changed. For better or for worse, I would never be the same again.

"Do it."

Both Sebastian and Zeus looked at me. I turned around in Sebastian's arms, facing him to convince him he had to do this. "Inherit me." Sebastian's eyes bored into mine. He read me, searching for my meaning. "Choose me, Sebastian, and don't allow these humans to control my fate. I want you. I've chosen you, and you told me forever. Make good on your promise."

I expected his reaction to be a lengthy argument, trying to save me from a destiny I was being forced into. I expected him to refuse me and demand I fight for what was right. But what I had forgotten was how Sebastian accepted and embraced what he considered to be beautiful—being a wolf.

His kiss told me so many things: How much he loved me, how much he admired me, how much he wanted me, and how much he wanted *this*. Sebastian pulled my body to his and held me so tightly. "Oh, Marley, you honor me with your request. When Zeus told me we wolves have very long lives, my first thought was of you and how I would survive witnessing your death of old age. I know I could not, and now I don't have to."

He kissed me with longing and hope I felt deeply.

Sebastian looked at Zeus without letting me go. "My cousin, I ask you… how?"

Zeus said, "When we came for you, I was in a pack of six."

"The six originals…" What the man in unit six had said now made more sense. But there were many more wolves now.

"In an effort to save the five fated to travel with me, I did what they asked me to do and inherited more males—men brought here against their will. I refused the females because without a mate to introduce them into a pack, the females would be left on their own—as good as dead in our world. I could not mate them because we mate for life. Your uncle willingly changed the females, but none survived the experiments they were forced to endure. That is why Boss was so pleased with your offer to inherit Marlena. He thinks because of your size, you are stronger. He is right, but not for the reasons he believes. It's your essence. With it, Marlena would've survived the testing and helped Boss learn more about us."

"Then why change his mind?" Sebastian asked.

Zeus ran his hand down his face. "Your uncle convinced Boss that the moon is coming to full strength and will change his normal outcome and that Boss would have more control over Marlena if your uncle were to be her alpha."

Sebastian growled.

Zeus smirked. "Clearly, you do not agree with this arrangement."

"And my uncle's reason for choosing Marlena?"

Zeus sounded saddened. "To control *you.*"

Silence.

"My Achilles heel." Sebastian repeated Boss's words before kissing my head.

Zeus looked to the surrounding wolves. Knowing they could hear a whisper from quite a distance, he quietly told them, "I know how the ones I travel with feel, but out of respect for the ones forced into this life, I must ask… By inheriting Marlena tonight—tomorrow, we go to war."

Again, snouts rose to the moon in a silent howl. Zeus smiled. "I am proud to call you my brothers." He looked back to us. "So be it." Then with his shoulders rolling back with pride, he told Sebastian, "Become your wolf, my leader."

Chapter Eighteen

Sacred Moments, Songs of Death

ROMY STARED AT ME WHILE Zeus guided us. "Most choose to be bitten in the thigh or the waistline—more meat there to handle the canine teeth. Which would you prefer, Marley?"

"Will I scar?" I refused to break eye contact with Romy. We were connected.

"Yes, but most find it to be a symbol of their rite of passage."

I thought of Agatha's scar on her leg and then proudly said to Romy, "I want to carry your mark on my waist."

Zeus bowed his head, and all the wolves turned away. "This is a sacred moment for only the chosen and the one to inherit. My words will guide you, but I will not watch so you two may bond in the most personal way a wolf can invite you into his life. Kneel, dear Marlena, for it is time."

I dropped to my knees in the snow with no hesitation.

"Sebastian, son of Mercio, lie on your stomach where you now stand." Zeus was sure to use our proper names. Romy's belly went to the snow with his paws in front of him. "Tonight, we share the moon with Sebastian and Marlena as they unite." Without raising his eyes to see us, Zeus told me, "Marlena, daughter of Everett and Amelia, remove your shirt."

I had requested my mother's name be mentioned, even though it was not custom.

I removed my shirt, proudly exposing myself to my wolf, waiting for instructions.

"Sebastian, to make this a non-aggressive event, I'm asking you to crawl to your Marley."

Romy's back paws pushed him forward as his front paws pulled on the snow in front of him. As I watched this submissive, majestic animal approach me, I instantly understood why. Romy looked kind and gentle, and it helped reduce the fear of allowing such a powerful animal to bite me.

Encouragingly, Zeus said, "Sebastian, your saliva is key for this bond. You must consume all your mouth can encompass. To show your respect for the one allowing you into her being, lick the front of her, right above her hip, and repeat the process on her back."

As Romy stayed in a prone position, he easily reached my waist as his mouth opened and licked me across my belly to my side. I whispered, "I love you." Another long lick came across my back to my side.

Zeus spoke again. "Don't be afraid, Marlena. Your mate is of strong blood. His essence will guide you. Sebastian, open your mouth and place it over the area."

It was amazing to feel and witness the size of Romy's jaw. Almost my whole waist was inside his mouth that was being as gentle as a baby's.

"Sebastian, close your eyes and connect with the power you feel around you. Trust your essence to know what to do, and commence your union."

Sebastian's eyes closed with me inside his mouth. Soon, I felt something move around him, around me. It was like a cleansing breeze, yet there was no physical movement. I inhaled freely as my soul filled with light and my heart with love. I became so entranced with what was happening around me, inside me, that I didn't even feel pain as his mouth tightened around my waist, his teeth sinking into my skin. I simply felt overtaken in a magical bliss. I surrendered with no fight.

I did not know I was moving downward. The only reason I had any knowledge was because Zeus quietly said, "Don't release her… follow her… lie with her."

The snow next to my face was the last thing I saw as my wolf held my body in his mouth and lay next to me, sharing his essence.

"Sebastian?" I woke, fully clothed again.

Lips brushed mine. "I'm here. You slept all day, Marley."

My eyes opened. Early evening air welcomed me. I felt rested and touched his face, hovering over mine. Sebastian kissed my palm the way he always had—the way he always will.

"I love you," I told him softly. His eyes closed as his face so affectionately caressed my hand. I whispered, "When?"

"Don't know. He says it's different for all." Sebastian was talking in code again, so no humans passing could overhear and understand us. I felt like I could sense Sebastian's emotions—or some sort of impression of his present state of mind. It was amazing to sense someone's well-being so purely.

The night got darker as I stayed in Sebastian's embrace, continuing to silently communicate, silently branding each other. It was a phenomenal experience. With my arm around his neck, I pulled myself to him. "I feel you inside me."

His whisper was so quiet I didn't know how I was hearing it. "I know. I felt your blood travel through me, Marley, and join with my... everything inside me and beyond."

We stayed that way for as long as we could.

Zeus, in wolf form, growled, maybe because of the approach of ones who meant us harm or maybe because our battle was soon going to escalate, and some would die.

Footfalls echoed miserably inside my ear. "Isn't this romantic? The *moon*—lovers holding each other," Boss cooed. I heard his voice with a new vibration, one that lightly scraped my flesh, like a cheese grater. And his odor was nothing if not totally offensive. Boss continued to assault my ears. "Too bad I have to break it up, but we have quite an eventful evening planned. Took all day, but the time is finally here."

Wolves breathing... I could actually hear exhales and inhales of wolves cages and cages away from mine. I heard wolves on the other side of the tents barking.

Men surrounded our cage; the smell of their leather boots told me so. Sebastian and I kept staring at each other. I kissed him, heedless of the many witnesses, as noose poles took their positions. Sebastian kissed my forehead, and we stood up *together*. I stepped to his back, as Sebastian turned from me to lean forward and place his head through the waiting wires. My eyes closed as I inhaled, begging myself not to attack every human around me.

I sensed the moon caressing me. That was when I knew the change was coming soon. Everything sounded so intense. The blood in my veins burned with so many desires to protect my *mate*. My shoulders rose and fell as my breathing became labored. Wolves howled. I could sense them sensing that I was becoming one of them.

"Look at me," Sebastian gently said. I hadn't even realized he had turned in his noose to face me again. My *soul* reacted to his command. My eyes opened, and even in the dark, I could see details in his gaze I never thought possible. "You with me, Marley?"

"More than ever."

"Am I going to have problems with you, *human*?" asked Boss.

Yes. "No."

"Need to tie you up? Or are you going to follow this mutt like a good girl?"

I will follow him to the end of time. I walked submissively behind Sebastian. I was simply waiting, like the rest of my new family, for an opportunity to present itself.

Boss suspiciously watched me. "Keep a gun on her forehead. Lycan, one move? She's dead. Let's go."

More nooses went around Sebastian's neck as the others released. I grabbed Sebastian's hands that he held behind his back. With ten men armed and surrounding us and floodlights shining from temporary power poles, Sebastian and I were led around the bend. Wolves growled the whole time. Now I understood. I felt their rage, witnessing their leader being treated so disrespectfully. It was against their—*our* natural order.

It was shadowy, but I could see my father pacing in the back of a larger cage, attached to a row of other connected cages. The cage next to my father's contained a snarling Maximus, Sebastian's uncle. Not leaving Sebastian's back, I said, "Dad!"

I was relieved to see him still alive, even though something felt... off.

My father stopped pacing and smirked. "Good evening, little girl."

I was surprised when a chill ran up my spine. The guards took us to his pen, opening my father's gate. My father stepped out of a shadow, spreading his arms. "Come hug your daddy."

I began to take a step around Sebastian but stopped when I heard his growl, his command. Sebastian's voice was gravelly. "Marley, stay with me."

Boss started laughing. "Very good, wolf. That was quick."

My father grinned some more, letting his empty arms fall.

From behind him, I asked Sebastian, "What is it?"

Sebastian started to turn and answer me, but his nooses tightened, silencing him and keeping him from facing me completely. Maximus and the wolves next to my father's cage made noises resembling hyena laughs. Sebastian was still struggling with the tight nooses, but his arms found me, pulling me protectively to him. I leaned into Sebastian's chest as I looked around, blocking blinding floodlights from my newly sensitive eyes with my hand, trying to figure out what I was missing.

"You love him now," Boss told me, "but will you love him twenty minutes from now?"

Always and forever.

Sebastian was pushed by the poles restraining him, which forced us both inside my father's area. Nooses were released, and the gate was locked behind us. Sebastian speedily grabbed my face. "Marley, remember him for *all* the wonderful things he did *all* your life. Never forget the man who has adored you and showed you that love with every kind action—"

"No," I said as I began to understand my father's forced promise. *"Choose Romy…"*

Sebastian ignored me. "Don't forget how a *bad* essence can change who you *were.*"

"No!"

"I'm so sorry, Marley."

"NOOOOOO!"

Boss laughed. "Oh, but it is true. Thanks for the *essence* tip. I'd been wondering why such a dramatically different wolf would come from this wolf versus the other one, but watching a proud man fight losing himself has been one of my most favorite experiments to date."

My body jumped to attack the man mocking my pain, but strong arms caught me midair. Boss smiled and continued to poke at my fresh wound. "Whoa! Is there fight in this human after all?"

I'm not human, you asshole!

His laugh made my skin burn. "Oh, your father pleaded and begged for a different outcome as his *soul* was ripped from him."

I kicked at the cage between me and the man I hated most. It was all I could do because Sebastian was not letting my feet touch the ground, preventing me from finding the traction needed to rip the cage apart.

Boss laughed and laughed.

161

I growled. "I will find pleasure in your death."

There was another laugh, but it wasn't from Boss, and it made the hairs on the back of my neck stand and warn me. Sebastian slowly turned, still holding me, to face the man I had admired and respected since I understood how lucky I was to have him. But that man was gone, and what stood in front of me was a creature who seemed to hold hatred. My heart cracked, and my chest ached in measures that compared to what I'd experienced during my mother's death.

He whispered so only the wolves could hear him. "We know what you two have been up to... *last night.*"

Boss stepped forward. "I couldn't hear that."

Sebastian set me back on my feet, quietly begging my father, "Don't do this," as he forced me behind him.

My father's eyes shifted from his blue to the same scary electric green as Maximus's eyes. "Romy, coming out to play with me?"

I quickly turned to Boss. "You're going to make them fight?"

"Nah, too easy. I'm having your father try to kill *you*, so your big, bad wolf will protect you. I love to test lines that shouldn't be crossed. Like I said, you *love* your fleabag now, but will you when this is over?"

Boss knew my father didn't have a chance battling with a wolf of Romy's stature. Boss wanted to witness *me* witnessing my father's death. And my father had tried to warn me. The bandage on his arm. Maximus. His words. "*Choose Romy.*" He knew what was going to happen to him, yet he still put me first, tried to protect me until he couldn't anymore.

My father's clothes exploded into the air as he morphed into a mangy brown wolf, right in front of my eyes. I didn't even have the chance to mourn the loss of my daddy before he lunged for me. Sebastian's arms were around the wolf's neck with an unnatural speed. He had my father down to the ground in a headlock, looking just as surprised as I.

Zeus had told us Romy was not aware of his powers. Light was being shed on that statement, and Romy was merely in his human form. I knew my father, even as a wolf, stood no chance going head to head with Romy at full strength.

Sebastian must have realized this, because he was telling my father, "Please, don't make me do this!"

I became hysterical as I was faced with a choice no one should ever have to make. I had to decide whether or not to allow my lover to kill my father, or to allow my father to kill me, which I knew Romy would not stand for. Either way, someone was dying in this cage.

I turned to the fencing and shook it while screaming at Boss, "You're the devil!"

I heard the wolf my father had become growling and trying to attack Sebastian. I could hear Sebastian's human form struggling against the power of the wolf that did not wish to be contained. He needed to become Romy, but that meant the balance would no longer exist.

I looked to the dark sky and screamed, begging for mercy, mercy that would not come. In moments, my father's blood would be spilled. There was no going back. My mother had been shot and killed in front of me, and now I was going to be forced to watch my last parent, my last human blood member, be ripped from my heart by the man I loved.

My throat was raw from my bloodcurdling screams of terror, but the time had come, and the decision needed to be announced. My choice must be revealed.

With my back to the horror, one last scream was forced from my lungs, "*ROMY!*"

I heard Sebastian crying, and I realized I had the easy part. I didn't have to murder the man who had loved me and watched me grow into the man who would bring his death.

"Don't watch, Marley!"

I clung to the fencing as my body shook violently, and I closed my eyes. Sebastian's voice was replaced with Romy's tortured growls. I felt the two wolves behind me. Their paws pounced and gripped the earth, the earth that vibrated like a song of death.

A wolf's whimper told me the deadly bite had taken place.

Then... silence.

No howls. No laughter. No sounds of my father's breathing. He was gone.

My knees gave out from under me as my heart shattered into pieces. I fell to the ground, slumped up against the fence. Boss knelt in front of me, and the son-of-a-bitch smiled. "You don't look to be in love anymore, *little girl.*"

Boss jumped back as Romy lunged at the fencing. I wish I could say

Boss was offended, but he wasn't. He was joyously boasting in his success. "You just killed her father! Can she ever look at you again? Are you scared, *Lycan?*"

Romy's head dropped in shame. Boss was playing his most disgusting game to date.

I cried and shouted to Boss, "You gave him no choice, you bastard!"

"This is true. But will you ever forget your father's blood dripping from your wolf's mouth… like it is now?"

I slowly looked to a painfully shameful Romy. His fur was matted with my father's tainted blood. "No, I will never forget, but…" I looked at Boss and began to play my own game. "I still love him. In fact, for his sacrifice, I love him even more."

Romy's head rose with my words. He dared face me when he understood I could not and would not hold him responsible for a madman's insanity. Romy slowly came to me. I leaned to him and wrapped my arms around his neck. I looked at Boss again. "Forever."

Boss rushed the fencing between us with pure hatred in his eyes. "That's what *she* said!"

Something was making Boss crazy. Spit flew from his mouth as he yelled, "What is it with these mangy dogs and loyalty from women who have lain with them? I will get to the bottom of their power over you, and I will save my son!"

"She? Your son?" I was so confused.

"*MY* SON!" he screamed with lunacy. "Don't you question me! He's *mine!*"

"What does your son have to do with the wolves?"

"My son is the result of his mother being a Lycan-loving whore. So far, my beautiful boy is still human. I will not allow him to turn into one of these creatures from the bowels of hell. And if he does, I will save his soul and have a cure waiting."

"You're torturing these beings to learn how to prevent a possibly unpreventable transformation?"

"He is pure and innocent. He deserves a chance to stay that way."

"Can't you just love your son for what he is?"

Madness erupted inside Boss. "NO! 'Cause then he will resemble his—" Boss almost admitted what we all knew now. This boy he spoke of was indeed *not* his.

I felt satisfaction. I had won that round. "His mother and *true* father will save him from you, you lunatic."

"That is where you are wrong. I killed her *and* the miserable Lycan."

I gasped. That poor boy was trapped with the devil's finest tool.

Boss's expression went blank. He was completely unreadable as backed away. I waited to see his next move. I waited to see what chess piece he would pick next.

He said one word. "Proceed."

One of his guards walked away from Maximus, passing us and six more cages with similar-looking wolves in them, stopping at the seventh one. He pulled a lever, a side door rose, and the wolf walked through the opening into the adjoining cage. A cage with *another* wolf waiting. They both nipped at each other and then turned to face the next cage and us. The guard also headed toward us, walking to the next cage and pulling another lever. The two wolves passed through the opening to join the next wolf, also waiting.

This repeated until seven mean wolves, including Maximus, stood waiting for the last lever to be pulled. They waited to enter the cage that Romy and I were in.

Well played, Boss. Well played.

CHAPTER NINETEEN

FINAL LOSS

MY HEART POUNDED SO LOUDLY, I couldn't say whether the other wolves were reacting, or whether or not our new family was trying to help us. Romy stood in front of me, viciously growling at the wolves anxiously waiting to join us. As powerful as my wolf was, I was sure we were facing our demise.

Boss said, "Don't kill her. Just change her. The wolf? Tear him to shreds."

The wolves facing Romy and me paced, as if dying to get this fight started. They already knew I had been inherited and didn't seem to care. I guessed that was because Maximus's true goal wasn't to use us as Zeus had thought, it was to kill us.

Even under the floodlights, I could feel the moon shining on me, feeding me. My ears began to ring. Everything around me swayed in and out of focus. I stumbled and collided into Romy, as if on a moving ship. My legs tried to hold me up as all the cells inside me began to shift, realign, reorganize and guide me to be… reborn.

It felt like falling peacefully through clouds as I began my fall to the ground. It felt like heaven caught me as Sebastian's arms came around me, controlling my descent. He placed me gently to the cold ground and, over and over, whispered, "Embrace your calling. Embrace your calling. Embrace your calling…"

The words were like an unseen map for the final step that I had to take, a final message before surrendering to an unknown.

I did just that. I surrendered.

The pain Romy had experienced with his transition was not for me to endure. I slipped effortlessly and elegantly into the magical being I would be until the day the source decided. When my eyes opened, it was as if I was looking through a new pair of eyes.

I guess I was.

I heard Boss screaming, "No!" in the background while I took to my paws for the very first time. *Surprise, asshole.*

I expected to be unsteady, like Romy had when he first became Sebastian, but that was not how I felt. I felt sturdy as the boulders I used to play on as a child. I felt solid. I felt *whole.* I honored my need to shake my newfound fur, and it was a freeing act. I looked at my paws and saw white, but it was not the snow I was seeing—it was me. I was a magnificent white wolf. My head rose to see a naked Sebastian fall to his knees in bewilderment. "You're beautiful, Marley. Your blue eyes…"

He was entranced in human form, in such awe that he never heard the gate rise behind him. A purely natural, territorial instinct had me leaping over my true soul mate to stop the first wolf coming to attack him from behind. My mother had been ripped from my life, and my father had been stolen. No one, wolf or man, was taking Romy from me.

It was incredible to feel my body react in another form. I had just been a human and was now effortlessly leaping through the air after being on all fours. My new self reacted as a highly efficient, programmed machine. My wolf form knew exactly how to soar toward her target, as if I had practiced this action many times before. That was when I realized: I had not, but Romy had. The white wolf I had become was *truly* part of Romy and his essence. Once again, he was guiding me into the unknown.

Easily, my canines homed in and sank through fur, flesh, then to bone. The fur mingled with my tongue while unfamiliar scents filled my brain with information: what wolf I was biting, where he had been and who he'd been with. With so much racing through my mind, I was surprised it wasn't impossible to complete the task at hand.

The hardness of the bone between my canines only made my jaw insist on pressing down harder, until I heard a crack of its surrender to the pressure. The taste that filled my mouth told me I had executed a life-threatening injury. I may not have killed this animal at that very moment. But the history lesson my new taste buds somehow already knew told me this wolf—in time—would eventually die. An injury such as this one would prevent this wolf from defending himself in the woods.

The first bite *I* received was nothing like the gentle one Romy gave to inherit me. This one showed the power behind such intense animals. I expected to feel my own bone give way, but was not subjected to such torture. Sebastian had become Romy, and Romy had become my savior. The wolf was pulled from my back and flung into the air to the front of the cage to face the wrath of Romy. And wrath it was.

With me clearly being the lesser threat, four of the remaining wolves simultaneously turned on Romy. I watched in disbelief as they brutally attacked him. I tried to intervene but was stopped when another set of powerful jaws clamped down around the back of my neck, pulling me to the back of my father's prison.

Every struggle I attempted ended with me injuring myself further. Since he was not proceeding in his attack on me, it became apparent that the one holding me had other plans. I was forced to wait and witness Romy cry out with every bite he received. That was when I noticed the scene taking place behind Romy. I only looked away from Romy for a few seconds, but I saw and heard so much. Alarms blared, Boss yelled orders, and guns were being nervously aimed at free wolves, cages completely dismantled.

A wolf attempted to take down a guard but was unsuccessful. My heart cried for the wolf as he was shot in mid-flight, but then my heart found hope as Zeus appeared right behind the fallen wolf, leaping into the air. Zeus flew until his body crashed into the unprepared guard, sending him plummeting to the ground. His teeth snapped down on human flesh with precision. The guard didn't stand a chance against the expert attack.

More wolves ran toward bullets with a bravery I'd never witnessed before. The newer wolves showed impressive signs of the essence they'd inherited from Zeus.

Romy, on the other hand, was trapped in the cage with me. There were no friendly wolves to help with the wolves attacking him, but he no longer cried out with each bite because no more bites were being given. His absolute lineage, his dominating size, and his determination were being tested, a test he refused to fail—did not seem capable of failing.

Watching Romy attack, I realized he positively had no equal. I hadn't comprehended that his heart and soul were designed to lead until that very moment. I had just believed Romy was simply *special* and had a beautiful way of viewing life. *Now* I saw that Romy guarding my home, *his* home, was a result of his natural, deep-rooted instinct shining through. And this instinct was falling in line with the responsibilities he, unknowingly, was born with. Romy's body was designed to protect his pack by ferociously killing any threat.

A crushing blow from Romy's front paw took one of his attackers down, and then he quickly bit and broke the lesser wolf's neck. The wolf holding me with his canines began to tremble as we both witnessed the massacre.

Outside our cage, wolves began to take the upper hand, killing the humans that had been so cruel to them. Boss was bloody and slumped over, leaning against the cages he had forced us to endure.

On the inside of our prison, one by one, the remaining wolves met the same fate as the last and were violently killed by Romy. Looking at all the dead wolves lying on the ground, I realized who I *didn't* see. When Romy slowly faced me, his menacing body language told me he also knew who had me in his jaws. Maximus.

Romy had blood dripping from most parts of his body, some his own, mostly others'. His huge canines were completely exposed while his lips curled. The warning Romy executed was scary enough, but when John appeared behind him, unlocking our cage, fear was the least of Maximus's problems. Zeus, Agatha, and what I presumed and sensed to be the four other originals entered, standing proudly with their leader. The rest of the wolves respectfully circled the entrance but were not interfering in this family matter.

With no other option and knowing he was at the end of the revenge he had lived for, I believed Maximus chose to take one more victim before his ultimate surrender.

When his jaws tightened, causing irreversible damage to my neck and my breathing to cease, I transformed into my human form. In the midst of the confusion of what was happening to me, I was thankful that Sebastian and I'd had a few stolen moments to express our love and to say our goodbyes. My eyes bored into Romy's, pleading with him to live on and lead the werewolves after my passing. My tears were not shed for me or the losses I had tragically experienced in the recent days. They were for the beautiful grays that were refusing to let me go.

Time may have stopped or shifted into another reality as Maximus was charged. Seven wolves besieged him, and I was on the ground, within close quarters of being trampled. Maximus gave a hell of a fight, preoccupying the wolves trying to save my life. I pulled myself forward out of the chaos with my shaky arms.

I could feel my gift, the essence Romy had inherited me with, leaving my body. It made me hysterical. My heart bled for the final loss I was about to suffer. Wanting to respect all that Romy and Sebastian had ever been in my life, I clawed at the ground to escape the horrid captivity so that my final loss would not be shared with the darkness that consumed my parents.

John's black leather boots appeared before my eyes. I looked up at him and cried out for mercy. "Get me out of this fucking cage! *Please* don't let my last moments be in this confinement!" My body was lifted and moved, as I cried, "I don't want to lose him in that hell."

Gently, John laid me on the ground, covering my naked body with his jacket as Maximus howled out his final cry. I grabbed at my bleeding wounds, trying desperately to contain the last ounces of Romy's essence inside me.

When Sebastian appeared at my side, Zeus was speaking in his ear. I hoped he was sharing supportive words. I was thankful that Sebastian would have Zeus and his found family to help him survive losing me.

I reached to touch Sebastian's beauty one more time, just like his mother had, and my mother had with me. His hand held mine to his face as he kissed my palm, inhaling me for the last time. His smile was kind and gentle when he whispered, "Heal."

Tears fell to the ground as I admired his unrelenting courage. Through overwhelming sadness, I told him, "I wish I could… I love you… Forever, Sebastian."

With a dignified, prideful smile, Sebastian nodded, kissing my hand one last time. Then he spoke remarkable words. "I am your alpha, and I'm commanding you to transform and *heal*."

Without my permission, my human body conformed and became a wolf. And then…

The flame's shadows dance across my face as I watch our fallen burn in the fire we set. Ashes of their remains float up into the cold winter wind, never to be seen again. My feet are in snow that no longer feels cold to me, nor does the evening air.

Now, memories of the love that withstood the test of time and brought me here grace me as the flame's shadows dance across my face and show me I'm to have no regrets. Sebastian is right. We are *not* alone, and all this, even this loss and heartache, has purpose. Events causing violent shifts were created to make my heart one of the strongest. I stand proudly and wisely to the fact that I'm meant, in this very moment, in this very place, to bring change and understanding.

That's life: many levels of emotions, confusions, violence, needs…and *feelings*.

Love.

This knowledge has me feeling a sense of pride that I have never experienced before. An unbelievable kinship is forming with the wolves that surround me. Their fur blows in the cold wind as my father's body finds freedom in this night's fire.

I once read, *"Life is not your right, it is your gift."*

I promise, here and now, to always remember and treasure the gift that has been bestowed upon me. Because now I'm a wolf and have learned the cruel lesson of what can happen when fear owns mankind, when love for other beings is forgotten, and when respect for all life is not given.

"So we will meet with you in two weeks?" Sebastian asks John, the guard I will never forget.

I continue to stare into the fire as John answers, "Yes, after I retrieve Boss's son, I will meet you. I hope I'm doing the right thing."

Zeus had explained to us how Boss's son was born human because his mother was one. He also explained that this innocent boy would be transforming into his new form around the same age that Romy became Sebastian. Eleven or so. John told us the child is now ten.

Finally, my trance breaks to assure John of the importance of what I had asked him to do. "There is an innocent child out there, and he is one of us. No matter who his father was, he deserves a chance, and we're the only chance he has."

John looks at the ground. "I can't return, not after kidnapping a child."

Zeus touches John's shoulder. "It would be an honor to call you brother."

John deeply inhales and nods, knowing he will soon be the Lycan he was trained to hate. Boss's mysterious millions of dollars could only reach so far and create only so much destruction until God, the source, once again found balance.

Sebastian, holding my hand, kisses me deeply, telling me it is time.

My white fur blends with the snow and is accented by Romy's dark-gray fur.

One by one, wolves turn from the fire and into the night to begin the journey through wintery mountains, until we reach Canada and the rest of our family. Turning away from the flames feels like I'm leaving my old life behind. I guess I am. I allow my heart to rest with the knowledge that someday I will be with my parents again. God will make sure of it. Until then, we head into the night—*my wolf and me.*

Epilogue

"Thank you"

JIMMY WATCHED AS TREVOR HUNG yet another 'missing' poster. Guilt was eating him alive because his tracking gifts failed him during his most important search ever. After they had not heard from Marlena and no one had answered her phone, Trevor and Jimmy were the first to find Amelia's body. Police searched but came up with nothing but dead ends. Marlena, her father, and her wolf, Romy, had simply disappeared.

"Maybe we should tell them the truth," Jimmy suggested.

Trevor turned to his friend on the sidewalk. "Hound, and say what? We want a first-class trip to the loony bin?"

Jimmy knew Trevor was right. How would they explain what they saw—what they knew? They couldn't, so they didn't.

"I'm sorry," Jimmy quietly said.

Trevor put his staple gun in his other hand that was carrying posters and put his arm around his childhood friend. They walked toward Jimmy's truck. "The snow, Hound. Too much snow kept falling for you to keep that trail."

"But I was so close!"

"I know. It will haunt us both for the rest of our lives if we don't find her."

That thought spooked both young men. Not knowing what had happened to their best friend was something they would never get over, and that was why they searched and hung posters from town to town for two weeks. The media was forgetting about their missing friend, but Trevor and Jimmy would never have that luxury.

Trevor thought about the endless miles he and Jimmy had put on the little beat-up truck and how home didn't feel like home without *her*. Memories of Marlena were hauntingly everywhere as they passed through their hometown. Once through the last stop sign and almost home, Trevor leaned his forehead on the passenger window, anxious for a hot shower and a cold beer. Even beer reminded him of Marlena and Sebastian.

Before closing his eyes to shut out the constant memories, he yelled, "Stop!"

Jimmy slammed on the brakes and saw what Trevor was yelling about. Across an open field, Romy stood on the rim of the forest, watching them. Both young men jumped from the vehicle, ready to run and cross the field to reach the wolf, but stopped when they saw that Romy was alone. Romy being alone spoke of Trevor and Jimmy's worst fear: Marlena was gone. Both young men were unable to move as they stared helplessly at the gray wolf nervously watching them.

When Romy became a little restless, anxiously looking beyond the young men, Trevor and Jimmy both quickly glanced behind them. Seeing no one nearby but knowing Romy could probably hear someone coming, they raised their hands, begging. "No!"

"Please don't go—"

"We have to know—"

Trevor composed himself. "I don't know what happened to you, Romy, and you're probably scared and want to run, but," he whispered, knowing Romy could hear him, even with the distance between them, "is she—" Trevor couldn't complete the worst question in the world.

Jimmy choked out, "Alive?"

Romy searched behind the young men for danger, again then finally looked behind him into the woods where Trevor and Jimmy couldn't see. Waiting for Romy's reply was the longest moment of their lives.

Then the most beautiful white wolf with impossible blue eyes stepped from behind Romy. Trevor and Jimmy were stunned, wondering if it was possible. She was whimpering, wanting to hug her oldest friends.

Jimmy hesitantly whispered, "Mar-cakes?"

The white wolf barked *twice*.

Both boys went weak, falling into each other. Marlena was alive. They stumbled forward, needing to touch her, but a menacing growl warned them. Marlena nudged her aggressive wolf until he calmed.

Surrendering to the fact that Romy was scared for their girl, Trevor didn't attempt an approach but said, "We laid your mama to rest. She's okay."

Marlena whimpered again but was quickly soothed by Romy's nuzzling.

"I put flowers on her gravesite yesterday," Jimmy promised.

Sensing humans coming, Romy began to nervously pace behind the majestic white wolf. Keeping Marlena safe was his priority, for his heart and the survival of his pack.

A tear slid from Trevor's eye as he wholeheartedly said thank you to Sebastian for letting them see her.

Jimmy, grabbing his heart, was too emotional to utter his gratitude. He knew Romy was fighting his urge to protect Marley, yet still had brought her so that he and Trevor could have some peace. This simple gesture meant the world to Jimmy. He and Trevor could sleep again, knowing their dear friend was where she belonged, with the one she loved, the one who would die for her.

Suddenly, against Romy's wishes, Marlena ran forward toward her dear friends. Both boys watched her cross a field with such grace and strength, a powerful Romy easily keeping pace. Once to them, Marlena leapt up and knocked both young men to the ground with her front paws. Shocked faces were greeted with a lick each before Romy guided her away.

Stunned, Trevor and Jimmy sat on the ground, watching both wolves run back into the forest. Marlena stopped at the edge, taking in the sight of her friends for a beautiful memory. Trevor and Jimmy waved. Marlena and Romy disappeared. Both men hoped that someday they would learn what had happened that tragic night, and they both hoped for the chance to see Marlena and Sebastian again.

The horn beeping spooked Trevor and Jimmy. They didn't even hear the truck full of rowdy boys approaching. The truck slammed on the brakes, soil spraying from the old dirt road as Ted yelled out the window, "We've decided it's time you two became boneheads again and took a break from worrying. Come have some beer! And *girls*, of course."

T and Hound looked at each other, and for the first time in two weeks, they smiled.

Thank you so much for reading *My Wolf and Me*. This book has a special place in my heart. I even had a charm designed to represent Romy that is available on my website: http://indias.productions. These two young characters simply owned my soul for a while, and I hope you enjoyed their love as much as I have.

ABOUT THE AUTHOR

India R. Adams is an author/singer/songwriter, who has written YA and NA novels such as *My Wolf and Me*, *Blue Waters* (A Tainted Water Novella), *Steal Me* (A Haunted Roads Novel), *Rain* (A Stranger in the Woods Novel), and *Serenity* (A Forever Novel), as well as music for the *Forever* series.

India was born and raised in Florida but has also been lucky enough to live in Idaho (where she froze but fell in love with the small-town life), Austin, Texas (where she started her first book, *Serenity*, and met wonderful artists), and now Murphy, North Carolina (where the mountains have stolen a piece of her heart).

Being a survivor of abuse has inspired India to let others know they have nothing to be ashamed of. She has used her many years of professional theater experience to build characters and stories with dark undercurrents that stem from her personal life. She says, "I'm simply finding ways to empower perfect imperfections."

Another thing India feels needs to change is the problem of sexual slavery. She has joined forces with jewelers to design beautiful ways to raise money for nonprofit organizations. Even though India writes about serious subjects such as domestic violence, sexual abuse, and human trafficking, she has a magnificent sense of humor, as do her characters. Her novels are perfectly balanced between laughter and tears, letting readers see how to empower their *own* perfect imperfections.

CONTACT THE AUTHOR

http://indias.productions

Twitter.com/TheIndiaRAdams

Facebook.com/IndiaRAdams

Instagram: indiaradams

Facebook Group: Purple Flames

SPOTLIGHT ARTIST

Sitting at The Daily Grind in Murphy NC, I heard this young man, Wyatt Espalin, play live. The heart behind his performance had me thinking of Marlena's father, Everett. I imagined this organic folky sound to be what Everett would've been listening to on his back porch drinking his evening beer. Marlena's parents were such role models in my eyes, and I adore how much beta readers loved them. Listening to Wyatt had me thinking of another artist (a dear friend of mine and cowriter of the song "Shadows" for my *Forever* series) John Kelly. My favorite song of his is "I will love". This sweet song is one that represents both Marlena's parental figures—in a big way. That's when I realized who my next Spotlight artists would be.

In dedication to Everett and Amelia, readers, may I please introduce you to Wyatt Espalin and John Kelly.

http://www.wyattespalinmusic.com
http://johnkellysongs.com

Books by India R. Adams

Tainted Water
Blue Waters
Black Waters
Red Waters
Volatile Waters
Ashen Waters

My Wolf and Me

Ivy's Poison

Haunted Roads
Steal Me
Scar Me
Bleed Me (Coming Soon)

A Stranger in the Woods
Rain
River
Mist (Coming Soon)

Forever
Serenity
Destiny
Mercy
Hope (Coming Soon)

INDIA'S THANK-YOUS

First, I must thank the universe for the vision of a little girl being handed a puppy by a naked, injured woman. The intensity of the emotion between this woman and child created My Wolf and Me.

Ian Naster, you are so talented! Thank you for creating the wolf drawing and designing Romy's charm. (For those interested in this jewelry, please visit my website).

Thank you to Connie for helping with editing in the earlier stages.

Thank you to Sue for believing in this book from the beginning. I miss you.

Betaaaasssssss! Your input makes my books so much better! Just couldn't do this without you.

Thank you to my team at India's Productions for sometimes getting lost in the black hole of research and advertising but always finding your way back to me, hahaha.

To readers for allowing yourselves to fall in love with my characters.

To reviewers and Bloggers, for taking the time to share my work.

And, most of all, my family. I love you… infinity.

Made in the USA
Columbia, SC
31 May 2020

98791787R00104